Let the Women Have Their Say, a Trojan Novel

Richard Seltzer

BookLocker
Trenton, Georgia

Copyright © 2024 Richard Seltzer

Print ISBN: 978-1-958892-57-2
Ebook ISBN: 979-8-88531-721-4

All rights reserved. No part of this publication may be reproduced, stored in a retrieval system, or transmitted in any form or by any means, electronic, mechanical, recording or otherwise, without the prior written permission of the author.

Published by BookLocker.com, Inc., Trenton, Georgia.

The characters and events in this book are fictitious. Any similarity to real persons, living or dead, is coincidental and not intended by the author.

BookLocker.com, Inc.
2024

First Edition

Library of Congress Cataloguing in Publication Data
Seltzer, Richard
Let the Women Have Their Say: a Trojan Novel by Richard Seltzer
Library of Congress Control Number: 2024907880

Books by Richard Seltzer

Trojan War Fiction

Let the Women Have Their Say

Trojan Tales

We First Met in Ithaca, or Was it Eden?

Breeze

Shakespeare Fiction

Shakespeare's Twin Sister

We All Are Shakespeare

Other Fiction

The Bulatovich Saga: The Name of Hero

Meter Maid Marion, How to Tutor a Ghost, The Third Tortoise

To Gether Tales

Echoes from the Attic (with Ethel Kaiden)

Parallel Lives

Beyond the 4th Door

Nevermind

Saint Smith and Other Stories

Children's Books

The Lizard of Oz and Other Stories

Now and Then and Other Tales from Ome

Essays

Why Knot?

Jokes

Grandad Jokes

Translation (from Russian)

Ethiopia Through Russian Eyes

How to do business on the Internet

Web Business Boot Camp

Shop Online the Lazy Way

The AltaVista Search Revolution, two editions

Take Charge of Your Web Site

The Social Web

The Way of the Web

DEC (Digital Equipment Corp.)

Snapshots of DEC

MGMT MEMO: Management Lessons from DEC

Dedication

To Nancy for her inspiration, feedback, and patience, and also for her insights in *Regarding Penelope*.

Acknowledgments

To Rex Sexton and his widow Rochelle Cohen for decades of support and inspiration.

To Mike Levine for a critique that prompted a much-needed rewrite.

To Sandy Carlson for her feedback as a beta reader and for her podcast interview (Woodbury Writes on YouTube).

To Cynde Lahey of the Norwalk CT Library for her continuing support of local authors and independent publishers.

To Gabi Coatsworth for her writers' meetups and publishing advice.

To my son Tim for his advice on hand-to-hand fighting.

And to my son Bob for his continuing support.

Preface — Troy Wasn't Where You Thought It Was

Imagine you are in ancient Troy, facing the challenges and constrained by the technology, traditions, and knowledge of that time.

Women are the property of men, first of fathers, then of husbands. They often die in childbirth. Strangers are treated with great respect, as if they might be gods in disguise. Horses are for pulling chariots, wagons, or ploughs, not for riding. Neither the Greeks nor the Trojans have written language. (That comes hundreds of years later.)

And Troy isn't where you thought it was.

Since the days of Heinrich Schliemann 150 years ago, experts have located Homer's Troy at Hisarlik in the northwest corner of what is now Turkey, near the beginning of the Dardanelles, the waterway leading from the Aegean to the Black Sea. Based on that location, historians and novelists have presumed that the war was fought for control of that strategic sea passage.

By the time of the Trojan War, the Hisarlik site had been occupied for hundreds of years, one city built on the ruins of another. But the city of Troy in Homer's *Iliad* was founded on new ground by the grandfather of the present king. And it had no port — just a beach, and no fleet — no ships at all, not even fishing boats. When Paris wanted to sail to Sparta seeking Helen, ships needed to be built for the occasion, and not by a shipwright, but by a smith, a worker in metal (Book V, 59-63). Troy had little to do with the sea. Its trade and its allies were land-based.

So, imagine that Troy is about twenty miles southeast of Hisarlik, on the Edremit Gulf, across from the island of Lesbos and near Mount Ida, in a location without strategic significance, where it can thrive as the hub of land-based trade and alliances.

You are a participant, not just a witness. Open your mind to unexpected twists.

Part One — Bargaining with Gods

Chapter One — Destined to Change Destiny?

It must have been a dream.

But there's blood on the cloth beneath me.

He was godlike.

No, he was Apollo himself. And I dared to defy him.

I said no, but he insisted. So I bargained.

He asked what I wanted in exchange for complying.

I said, "Knowledge. Real knowledge. Knowledge of the future."

He objected, "That would overwhelm you. It would drive you mad."

I replied, "But if I knew, I could spread that knowledge to others. It could inform our choices. We wouldn't err from ignorance. We could change the future, for the benefit of all."

"You can't change the future. Everything is fated. What's the point of knowing it?"

"If it can't be changed, what's the point of living?" I asked him. "I want to change what otherwise would be, and help others do likewise."

"What irony! You want to exercise personal agency? That would disrupt the cosmic order. It would lead to chaos." He laughed. "Such ambition from a human, a female, no less? You can understand what happens in the here and now. You can cope and survive, one step at a time. That's all you can handle."

"Well, this *is* here and now," I told him. "So by your words, I already have freedom of choice. And I choose not to give myself to you."

"How dare you deny me! Such impudence!"

"How dare you force yourself on me and steal the modicum of freedom you say is all I have?"

"You make too much of this. A few moments of pleasure for me and for you, as well — intense pleasure, you can be sure. I am a god, after all. Take it. Enjoy it. And savor the memory for the rest of your all-too-short life."

"Only if you give me the gift of second sight."

"But it will drive you mad."

"So be it then."

"Then so it shall be," he laughed. "You will see the future ever so briefly."

"For however long, I must see. That's who I am and who I want to be."

"You're mad, my dear, to want such knowledge. What ambition! That's what draws me to you, a mere human. I'm fated to want you for that, as you're fated to ask for such a fate."

So I accepted him, and he entered me. And for a moment, I saw all of human history, past and future. It was a moment all-too-bright, a cosmic orgasm of knowledge.

For a moment, I knew everything. All I remember now is a jumble of images and sounds. How can I make sense of it? If I'm to change destiny, I have no idea how to do it.

Chapter Two — Family Matters

Lying beside Priam in their bedchamber, Hecuba thinks, I was lucky. Father didn't know the qualities of this man when he matched me to him. May our children have such good fortune.

I have given him sons and daughters, year after year; and by arranging their marriages, he has bargained for wealth and alliances, making Troy stronger than all our neighbors.

But family matters. Our daughters have a pedigree of fertility, my fertility; and all our children have our height, strength, wit, and resourcefulness. For all that, they command high prices. Priam focuses too much on politics. He should give more weight to blood lines and breeding. We breed horses, don't we?

A man should never look down on his wife, nor she on him. Looking shapes thinking. They should be well matched in height as well as temperament. It's not by chance that we have such tall, athletic children. If we choose the right mates for them, imagine the next generation.

Sometimes nature fixes what man would bungle. At the betrothal of Cassandra to Eurypylus, he was scrawny and pimply-faced, and he towered over her. She was a little girl despite her age. I told Priam he was making a mistake. He ignored me. The alliance with Mysia was important. But look at them now. Many say Eurypylus is the handsomest man in the world and Cassandra is his perfect mate. It's fortunate her first period has been slow in coming. That gave her time to sprout and blossom. Now she's at least as tall as he. And that's how he'll think of her and she of him when they finally marry — equals.

Family, yes, family. It matters that his grandfather was Heracles himself. That height. That build.

At that age, Priam was just as tall and handsome. That was before I was born. He's still a fine specimen, despite his age. Still potent. I think we made another son last night. That could be our last. The change will come. I'm only human.

Cassandra's period will come, too. No need to fret.

We should think of Hector. What woman is worthy to be his partner? And Polyxena? She'll have her growth spurt soon. Then we can focus on our children's children. Family, our ever growing family. Yes, family matters.

*****

Priam wakes with a start. He senses there's something urgent he needs to do. What's troubling him? Cassandra? Yes, Cassandra.

I must have had a dream, he thinks. May the gods grant that I not remember it. Dreams can be dangerous, like Hecuba's, so long ago. I should have forgotten it by now. Forgetting is supposed to come with age. But her dream still haunts me.

It frightened her so much she told it to my son, the seer. She forced him to explain what it meant. It was a warning from the gods. Our newborn, should he grow to manhood, would cause the destruction of Troy. So we let the baby be exposed, to die. Yes, we've had many others, but I remember that one as the handsomest and sweetest of them all. Alexander we named him.

May the gods grant that I not remember dreams, he thinks.

Then he explodes aloud, "Traditions be damned. Cassandra must marry without delay. We've waited long enough."

"But she's still a child," replies Hecuba.

"If I say she's ready, she'll marry."

"Since when are you a god?" asks Hecuba. "Let nature take its course. The remedies she tried didn't help. They may have prolonged the delay. Or maybe it's anxiety, from the way everyone looks at her."

"She has the body of a woman," Priam insists, "a beautiful woman, fully formed. Just this one small thing remains — a technicality. Eurypylus and his father find the delay unconscionable. They hear rumors that we're having second thoughts about the alliance or we're pressuring for a higher bride price. No wonder people say that. We betrothed them with great fanfare four years ago, and still she hasn't had her first blood. By my reckoning, she's ripe for marriage. She's a tempting morsel to any man who sees her."

"How can you speak that way about your daughter?"

"How can we not take action now? Let's tell Eurypylus the blood has come. Let's hold the wedding. There'll be blood enough on their wedding night. Then nature can take its course."

"Such hubris! You'd be challenging the gods and fate."

"The gods have more important matters to deal with."

"But the people and the priests, the force of belief and tradition?"

"What the people don't know won't hurt them. This very night, while Cassandra sleeps, I'll have Arisbe pour pig's blood on her bed. She can be trusted if anyone can. Then, in the morning, when handmaids find the blood, they'll spread the word. All of Troy will know by noon, Mysia by sunset. That ruse will be enough. We're not defying nature; we're giving it a boost. Nine months from their marriage, we'll have another grandchild. I can see it now. I feel the joy and confidence of a prophet. Cassandra will, like you, have one child after another, to her joy and ours, and to the joy of both nations."

Chapter Three — The Meaning of Blood

Pig's blood he wants? Well, so be it, thinks Arisbe. I'll not second-guess the King. If I were still his wife, I'd speak my mind. If the gods frown on such a ruse, let it be on his head. I'm a witness, not an actor. I'm here to do what I'm told to do and watch what comes of it. I'm not one of the high and mighty, deciding things for myself and taking the consequences.

Unlike most, I had my chance. He paid no bride price for me. His father was dead and gone. He was free to do what he pleased. He saw me. He took me. And I pleased him mightily. He told me as much. So he made me his queen.

He was generous to my father, but didn't need to be. He was king. I was his if he wanted me, marriage or no marriage. And he was so proud when I bore him a son that first year. But after that, none lived to birth. And when my change came, and there would be no more, he put me aside and took another as queen. I'd had my turn. It was time for someone else to have a go at it; and so she did — so many children from the same womb, and still she's the picture of health. The gods must have wanted it so.

He would have set me up with a life of leisure. But I told him I wanted children. They would be the love of my life. Since I couldn't have more of my own, I would care for his. I'd raise them and teach them. I'd second-mother them and be happy doing it.

I made the best of bargains. I love his children and they love me. And I have no risk of childbirth and don't need to fret about my looks and my aging. I flow with the current of life. I don't need to make history, just make beds, change diapers, and love the children. I'm more a mother to them than the woman who bore them, fine lady that she is, with no need to dirty her hands, so tall and regal. She looks like a queen. I never did. I never could.

I've not raised all of them. There are too many, and I'm only human. I pick the ones I want to raise. What more can a woman want?

Cassandra will be off to Mysia, or I'd raise hers too.

But Hecuba's not done yet. She's as regular as the moon, and she'll be having at least one more before her change. This time I hope it'll be a boy. Girls leave; boys stay. May I live long enough to see what comes of them, to share their joy and their children's joy.

Pig's blood — that's what he said. I've never dealt with pigs before. Foul creatures. But blood is blood. And whoever sees blood on her bedding, even she, will presume it's hers. It's been such a long wait.

So I'll do this business with the pig's blood and not worry my conscience over it. If it doesn't work, it's on his head, not mine.

*****

By the light of her candle, Arisbe notices blood on the cloth beneath Cassandra. The period came on its own! There's no need for trickery. The wait is over. Cassandra's life as a woman will begin.

Arisbe is about to awaken Cassandra and to deliver the good news. She'll exclaim her joy loudly to let the handmaids know. They'll let the household know, and from them the news will spread.

Then she sees bruises on Cassandra's thighs, hips, even shoulders. There's been a struggle. This was rape, but by whom? Who would dare rape a princess in her bed chamber? Who had such access? Who was capable of such a crime?

Cassandra wakes up. There's fear and confusion in her eyes. She reaches out for Arisbe and holds her tightly.

On Cassandra's breath, Arisbe detects the smell of wine and something else, too, perhaps a drug.

Cassandra pulls away, stands, paces, and talks, on and on.

"It was Apollo," she claims. "Olympian Apollo himself, the handsomest of the gods. He came here last night and forced himself on me. I fought him, with my nails and teeth. These bruises are nothing next to what I did to him. It's a good thing my brother Len and I wrestled so much when we were young. Some of that blood may be his, the blood of a god. So gods can bleed? No one ever told me that. I held him off. Then Apollo backed away and rather than force me, we bargained. What did I want that he could give me?"

"And what did you say to that?" Arisbe probes, indulging Cassandra in her fantasy, trying to calm her frenzy.

"I told him I want knowledge, true knowledge. I want to know rather than guess what will result from what we do today."

"And did he give you that?"

"He did, indeed. All in a burst. He flooded my mind with images and sounds. I had no time to think. It came at me too fast. But it's all there in my memory. Flashes come to me even as we talk. The images are overlaid on you and on the bed, the floor, the walls. It's as if there are two of me, one who sees the now, another who sees the future, in color, more real than real."

"And what did you make of it?"

"I don't know what the images mean. Maybe, over time, I'll be able to make sense of the vision and prevent bad things from happening."

"What bad things?"

"There will be war and death and destruction."

"Sounds like a dream your mother had soon after giving birth. It was a prophecy. If the newborn lived to grow up, he'd cause war and the fall of Troy. He was abandoned on the mountain to die. You know that story. It must have triggered this dream of yours."

"This wasn't a dream. It was real. You see the blood on my bed and the bruising on my body. And what I saw in exchange for my submission wasn't a dream. It was a vision, divine knowledge."

"Enough, my child, more than enough. I'll have warm broth made for you. I'll have handmaids bathe and massage you. But first I'll fetch your mother and father. They need to know what's happened and make their own sense of it, and decide what's to be done and who should know what. Lie down now. Please. I'll get them myself. Better that no one else hear of this before your parents."

"Bring Len as well, please. I have to tell him as soon as possible. We're as one. Maybe he can help me sort out who I am now that I've been with a god, and what I must do and say, regardless of the wishes and orders of our parents. I've been given a gift by a god, by Apollo himself. I have second sight. I am responsible not just to this family, but to the world. I asked for this knowledge. I suffered to get this knowledge. And now I must use it for the good of all. Bring me Len, please, right now, before my parents know of this."

"Yes, of course, I'll bring Helenus, if and when your parents let me. But I have to tell them first. Please rest. I'll be back soon."

"Rest? You think I can rest? My mind is racing. I feel more alive than ever before. I'll pace. I'll do handstands and cartwheels. Go quickly. Bring mother and father if you must. I want to get that over with so Len and I can figure out what this means — for me, for us, for the world."

Chapter Four — Priam's Take

Priam thinks Arisbe is mistaken about the bruises. The blood is from Cassandra's period, not from rape.

When he sees the bruises and hears Cassandra rave about Apollo, he's shocked. Is she mad? Or might a god have done this?

Cassandra paces back and forth across her bedchamber, talking to herself, repeating herself, trying to recall details of the vision.

"Fire everywhere," she says. "Bricks and even rocks are burning. The stink of rotting flesh. Tripping on corpses. Running from dogs feasting on corpses. The ground shakes as towers topple and crumble."

She mentions the names of her brothers, nearly all of them. Then she recites over and over again, "Achilles who is not Achilles."

"Achilles? Who's Achilles?" asks Priam.

When she doesn't reply, he tells Hecuba, "I've never heard such a name. It sounds Greek. But she's never met any Greeks. I've kept all my daughters away from Greeks ever since they kidnapped my sister and wouldn't return her at any price. Maybe, despite my orders, those two Athenian visitors met her, and she heard that name from them."

Standing on tiptoes, Hecuba kisses him on the chin and embraces him, then guides him to a corner by the chamber's sole window, where Arisbe joins them.

Priam continues, "What she claims about the future is vague. She doesn't say who the enemy is or when this will happen or why. Like Arisbe says, it sounds like an echo of your dream, Hecuba, distorted and expanded in the mind of an adolescent. She puts too much credence in myths and the talk of priests. Apollo raped her? That's nonsense. This was the work of a man. No, two men, those Greeks. The poor girl. Achilles! May Achilles be damned, whoever he is.

"We need to make sure word of this doesn't spread, be careful what we say and to whom. Her reputation, her marriageability, and the alliance with Mysia depend on how we manage the news. That's more important than blame, proof, and revenge. Those Greeks must leave before rumors start.

"Arisbe, take Cassandra to your bedchamber and tell no one that she's there. Say she has an illness that might spread. We're isolating her in an undisclosed place. Foreigners must leave before they're exposed."

Arisbe interrupts him. "On my way to you, I spoke to a guard who told me that the Greeks left in the night, without warning, without explanation. He wondered about that. He wanted you to know."

Priam interrogates all the palace guards, threatening torture and promising rewards for verifiable truth. He uncovers two who were bribed by Theseus, one for access to Cassandra's chamber and the other for nighttime exit from the city through the Scaean Gate. As proof, they show the bronze they were paid. Priam doubles that amount for their silence. The penalty, if they speak of this matter, will be death.

He tells Hecuba, "Rumor has it those same Greeks child-raped Helen of Sparta. That assault didn't diminish her marriageability. If word gets out that our Cassandra was forcibly raped, Eurypylus might still want her, and his father might still want the alliance. If that falls through, there will be other suitors, other alliances. In either case, I don't want to accuse the king of Athens. I don't want war over this. Better that the rapist remain anonymous. Better still that the public not know there was a rape. I don't want people gossiping about who did it and calling for revenge. Our story about a disease might preclude that. People will worry about their own health."

Hecuba notes, "She might be pregnant from this. But it will be months before we know."

Priam adds, "Her raving is a more urgent risk — her saying Apollo did it, the wild look in her eyes. Who would marry a mad woman? We'll keep her in isolation until she loses the compulsion to tell her god story and to claim she knows the future."

Chapter Five — Where's My Sister?

Helenus wakes up abruptly. Vivid, inexplicable images flood his mind. Scared and confused, he climbs the stone steps to the ramparts of the citadel and runs frantically. The images flip on and off, overlaid on the panoramic view around him — the plains full of warriors and the beach lined with hundreds of ships.

He has to talk to his twin sister Cass, Cassandra.

She isn't in her bedchamber or in any of the places she frequents. He goes to his own room and tries a game that they played as children. One of them would hide. The other would stretch out and try to think of nothing and hope to see and hear the other. It didn't always work; but when it did, it was like he was in her head and she in his. They would pretend that one of them had been kidnapped. They'd use this ability to find one another. Now he senses that she needs to be rescued for real. He has no inkling where she might be.

He asks handmaids and guards. They tell him that she's sick and might be contagious. She was playing on the beach when a caravan arrived from the East, bearing disease as well as goods. For her health and to prevent the spread, she's being kept in isolation.

He looks for his mother and father, but no one will tell him where they are.

He goes to the palace kitchen, where the freshest rumors can be heard. Theseus, king of Athens, and his friend Pirithous were lingering at Troy, taking advantage of Priam's hospitality. They were amusing themselves with handmaids, two or three of them at a time, paying them for their services. The pair left last night, abruptly, with no explanation, no farewell, and no departure gifts. Several of the handmaids are disgruntled, having been promised far more than they received. They say the Greeks bragged they had abducted Helen, the twelve-year old daughter of the King of Sparta, who already at such a young age was legendary for her beauty. They claimed to have had their way with Helen for weeks, before they tired of her and returned her.

Did they take Cass? Is that why she's nowhere to be found? Is the story of an illness a lie meant to mask that a search party has been sent after them?

Helenus wanders the corridors of the palace, listening at every door until he hears his father's voice. Then he pounds and screams, "Where is she? Where is Cass, my sister Cass? Has she been stolen by those filthy Greeks?"

Priam opens the door and pulls him inside. "She's being held in isolation," Priam begins.

Helenus finishes the sentence for him. "Because of some disease? That's nonsense. This has something to do with those Greeks from Athens, those pedophile rapists you welcomed here as guests. Tell me the truth. Did they take her? Can I go with the search party, to slit their throats and bring her back?"

"No one stole her, son. Your bravery is to be commended; but your sister is safe, here in the palace. Your mother and I have the situation under control. When we can tell you more, we will. And as soon as we deem that it's best for you and her, the two of you will be reunited. Patience, my boy. Patience."

"I will not be patient. If you don't tell me what's going on and where she is, I'll keep asking, and I'll pay whoever I have to pay to get answers and find her."

Priam and Hecuba exchange a look, then nod to one another. Priam says, "If you swear to tell no one, we'll share the truth with you."

"Just tell me. I'll swear anything."

"She's had an upset, an extreme upset," Priam continued. "She seemed to have forgotten who she is. She was raving gibberish that no one could understand. We drugged her to calm her, but that threw her memory into further disorder. When she was at her worst, to prevent her from harming herself we tied her up. She's with Arisbe now. In Arisbe's loving care, we hope she'll soon recover and go back to being her usual self. Then you can see her."

Helenus glares, unsatisfied.

Priam and Hecuba exchange looks again. Then Hecuba concedes, "We understand your concern. The two of you have a special bond. Maybe you would be good for her. You could calm her down and get her to change her story."

"What story?"

"She claims she was raped by the god Apollo."

"What?"

"It's nonsense, of course."

"So she was raped. That I believe. But not by a god. I wager those Greeks did it."

"We're concerned about her state of mind. She should know we don't blame her, regardless of what happened. We'll do all we can to protect her reputation. We'll see to it that she marries Eurypylus quickly, if possible. As you know, that's been delayed far too long."

"And if it turns out that she's pregnant, what happens then?"

"Yes, that sets a limit on how long we'll keep her in isolation. Since she hasn't had her first period, it'll be months before we know if she's pregnant. In the meantime, you can help. Convince her not to talk to anyone about what happened, except to you and us and Arisbe. And talk her out of her Apollo fantasy."

Chapter Six — Now I'm a Woman

"Len," Cassandra insists. "I never saw those Greeks."

"Well, they saw you, and that was enough. People heard them boast what they'd do to you if they could. It was them, not Apollo."

"Why the one or the other? Why not both? Maybe Apollo took over their bodies and attacked me through them. Maybe Apollo did the same to Helen. We know that gods can take the shape of men or beasts. That's why we honor strangers who come to the door. They could be gods in disguise."

"Well, if it was Apollo or any other god, why did you, as you say, make a bargain with him? Why did you give in?"

"Because I want to know the meaning of all things, not just their surface and semblance — their consequences. I want to know, rather than guess, what will happen because what we do today."

"Well did he give you what you asked for? What did you see? Tell me all that you can remember."

"A flood of images. The sound, the smell, the touch, the taste of death."

"Was it like mother's dream? Did you see Troy burning, sacked, its walls torn down, everyone slaughtered?"

"Yes, Len, I saw such horrors. I lived through them. But all in a burst. Now I see and feel it over and over again, in flashes, whether I'm awake or asleep."

"So if that was Apollo and what you saw was real, was the bargain worth it?"

"Only if I make it so. I have to understand what I saw and tell you, tell father, tell everyone. It's my mission now to prevent the destruction of Troy, to prevent those deaths. Knowing what's fated, I have to change it."

"If it's fated, how can you change it?"

"That's what Apollo said. But he's only a god. He doesn't know everything."

"And you're only a girl."

"No, Len. Now I'm a woman."

Chapter Seven — Healer of Mind and Body

"That was no dream," Aesacus tells Cassandra. His mother, Arisbe, asked him to interpret her ravings. "Many have asked me to interpret what they thought were messages from gods, as if the gods talk to everyone. I help heal their anguish by letting them talk about what's happening in their lives. I try to uncover the everyday causes of what troubles their sleep. Others come to me in my role as physician. As I examine their bodies, they tell me their dreams, thinking those might provide clues to their ailments. None of the hundreds of dreams I've heard have been like your mother's. Hers was true prophecy."

"But if mother's dream was prophecy, mine could be as well."

"Gods understand the limitations of the human mind, our inability to cope with a flood of divine knowledge. They'd never directly reveal the future to a mortal. They spoke to your mother using symbols. One thing meant another. And once I solved the riddle of correspondence, the message became clear."

"And you felt no guilt?"

"Guilt? What guilt? I helped to save our city and everyone in it."

"What you said led to the death of my brother, an infant, just a few days old. You have no doubts? No regrets?"

"You weren't there. You were born a year later. When you heard the stories, you imagined a helpless baby, murdered. Of course, you blamed me. But for me to do what I had to, I couldn't think of the infant as human. I saw that swaddled bundle as a harbinger of death and destruction."

"And so you persuaded his parents to kill him."

"Evidently, you don't know the details."

"They wouldn't talk about their role in the murder."

"It wasn't murder. They didn't lay a hand on it."

"A technicality. He was abandoned on the mountain, food for wolves."

"Once they knew the meaning of the dream, not just from me but confirmed by a priestess of Apollo, they could have let it die of thirst or exposure to the cold here in the palace. That's what I recommended. The priestess agreed that such a death wouldn't be their responsibility. But your mother didn't want to hear it crying. So, we gave it to the chief herdsman, to leave it, unattended on the slopes of Mount Ida, knowing it would perish there."

"Agelaus?"

"Yes. He was chief herdsman then, as now."

"I know him. He's a good man, a gentle loving man. I can't imagine him doing that."

"He did as he was ordered, as he had to."

"And you're sure the infant died?"

"Exposed like that, it couldn't possibly survive. And a week later, your mother asked Agelaus to return to the spot to be sure. He found the body just where he had left it, smiling, he claimed, spared by the beasts of the forest. He burned and buried the remains and brought back the severed tongue as proof of death. Your mother kept the tongue in a golden box by her bed, until it rotted to dust — thank the gods. Then she could set the memory aside."

"So you're an interpreter of dreams, a healer of minds as well as bodies. Well, then, decipher the symbols in my dream. And do it quickly. Please."

"What you've told me doesn't sound like a dream at all, much less a prophetic one. No symbolism. You saw Troy on fire, its towers and walls collapsing. Your senses became confused. You saw what you should have heard. You smelled what you should have felt with your finger tips. You experienced pain —your own and that of those who were dying around you. Images and sensations raced through your mind too fast for you to make sense of them. That's madness. You projected onto the world the agony you felt within. Maybe that was triggered by the rape, added to your anxiety about your delayed first period and the marriage that has been postponed so long. Regardless of the cause, you need rest and calm. I've brought a potion to help you sleep for a day or two. After that, focus on something that will help you forget that vision. Engage in a project that requires your full attention for an extended time. Weave a tapestry, replete with images from everyday life that have nothing to do with that vision of yours. Tell no one else what you saw, and don't repeat your account to those of us who've already heard it. When sensations from the vision invade your mind, prick your finger or stub your toe. Then focus on your project. Do anything to get your mind off that vision. Over time, with the help of the gods, you'll heal."

*****

In the months that follow, Cassandra weaves an enormous tapestry. With thread, she depicts disembodied heads, feet, hands, intestines, dripping in blood. Then she paints those over with bright colors, transforming them to familiar geometric shapes. On top of the paint, she makes marks with charcoal, and the shapes become irregular, random, not corresponding to anything in the real world.

Then, after three months, it becomes clear that Cassandra is pregnant.

Chapter Eight — Eurypylus

Secluded in Arisbe's chamber, Cassandra makes another tapestry, then another, lining the walls with them.

When she comes to term, the labor lasts a day and a night. Twin girls, both still-born. Cassandra is left exhausted and delusional. She screams when Aesacus, in his role as physician, takes the babies away. She imagines they are alive and will be exposed on Mount Ida and left to die, like her infant brother, Alexander.

Cassandra's breasts become swollen with milk, which aggravates her distress over the loss of her twins. Her mother, who conceived on the same day she did, soon delivers a healthy baby boy, Polydorus.

Arisbe sees this second birth as an opportunity. Cassandra could serve as wet nurse to her new brother. Aesacus agrees. That might help cure her madness.

Cassandra abandons her weaving, and Polydorus becomes the center of her world. Arisbe removes the tapestries and has them burned, so they won't give the newborn nightmares.

A year after the rape, Cassandra agrees to meet Eurypylus, who still wants to marry her. She waits for him in the megaron, the great hall of the palace. In that vast columned space, they are alone, except for the infant Polydorus, who is nursing at Cassandra's breast. Hecuba objected. "It's unheard of for a member of the royal family to breast-feed in public. What will Eurypylus think? Do you want to drive him away? I thought you wanted this marriage. Give me the child. You can have him back after you've secured your future." Cassandra waved her away, and Hecuba left, not wanting to bring on another fit of madness.

When Cassandra hears the double-doors open, she looks down at Polydorus, not wanting to meet the eyes of Eurypylus. This is her life she's deciding on. Her father has given her agency. She can marry this man or not, despite the fact that an important alliance hangs in the balance. Out of love for her, to help her heal, forget the rape, and forget her vision of the future, her father is letting her decide.

By choosing Eurypylus, she would please herself and please her father as well. Perhaps that's why Priam gave her choice. She has no reason to do anything other than take this man as hers.

His opening words are, "Is the child yours?"

"Rumor has it that he's mine. Does that matter to you? "

"Not at all. I've heard that you were raped."

"By a god, by Apollo himself."

"I heard it was a pair of Greeks, Theseus and Pirithous."

"Does that matter?"

"Not at all."

She forces herself to keep looking down.

Then he says, "You love that child, don't you?"

"Yes, I do," she answers emphatically.

"It doesn't matter to me whether he's yours or he's your brother, whether he's the child of Apollo or of Theseus. Bring him with you, and we'll raise him together."

She looks up and sees love in his eyes. This man respects her and will honor the power of choice her father has given her. He won't insist on his rights as her betrothed. He won't expect her to submit to his will. If she says *no* now, after he has waited nearly five years, he will feel pain and disappointment, but he will honor her choice. And if she says *yes*, she will be his equal partner. They can live together in harmony and with intimacy unlike any she has ever heard of between man and woman. With the confidence of a prophet, she knows that can be so.

That thought triggers her memory of Apollo's gift. The vision flashes before her eyes. In it, she recognizes Eurypylus. He's older, stronger, even more handsome. He's on a battlefield. There's a spear in his gut. He's dying in agony.

"No!" she screams.

"What?" he replies. "You won't have me?"

"No. I don't mean that *no*." She shuts her eyes and covers them with one hand, the other still cradling Polydorus at her breast. But the vision remains. In it, all motion has stopped. Eurypylus' life's blood is suspended in mid-air, seconds before his death.

She tells him, "Promise me that if war comes, when war comes — for surely it will — you will not fight for Troy."

"But our marriage contract includes the alliance of Troy and Mysia. If I marry you, I accept that alliance. I have no choice."

"Then you must promise me that you'll break the alliance."

"Why would you want me to do that?"

"Because I saw your death. I see it now in vivid color. The spear. Your blood. It's horrible. And I can't look at you without seeing it."

"You're talking like a madwoman."

"Like someone cursed by Apollo with second sight because I, in my hubris, asked Apollo for that gift."

"Apollo? You insist on that story? There's no need for you to keep up that pretense. I can accept that rapists had their way with you, and you love and wish to keep the offspring. But madness, madness like this? Tell me that's not so. Disavow that fantasy."

"If only I could. But the vision is fixed in my memory. I can't unsee it. And I can't bear to see you in such agony. Promise me you'll break the treaty. Maybe then the vision will fade, and I'll be able to look at you with love rather than fear."

He stares, then screams and runs off.

But even without the marriage, Eurypylus insists that his father ratify the treaty with Troy.

Chapter Nine — Cassandra Discovers Paris

Priam and Hecuba no longer mention Eurypylus to Cassandra. And at their request, Helenus and others do likewise.

Cassandra spends her days and a good part of her nights caring for Polydorus, delighting in her interactions with him.

When Polydorus is one year old, Cassandra takes him for walks on the slopes of Mount Ida. She favors the trails that lead to a grotto where a spring rises and forms a pool. She sits on a large flat rock, dangles her feet in the water, and cradles Polydorus in her arms, singing to him and telling him tales of gods, love, and war.

Sometimes a shepherd boy brings his flock to drink at the spring. He's shy. Their eyes never meet. They don't speak, though each waves a hand in greeting and parting.

One day the shepherd runs to the spring, without his sheep. He has a wild look in his eyes — a look of joy. He speaks to her abruptly, without greeting.

"I saw them. All of them. I really saw them."

"Who?" she asks.

"The goddesses. I knew they were goddesses even before they told me."

"Goddesses appeared to a shepherd boy on a mountainside?" Cassandra laughs, and Polydorus echoes her laugh.

The shepherd boy is a little older than she is, and up close, with a gleam of joy in his eye, he is very handsome. On impulse, Cassandra indulges his fantasy. "I, too, once saw a god."

"From a distance?" he asks.

"Up close, all too close, closer than close."

"He made love to you?" he asks.

"Yes," she says, laughing as if she's making this up.

"And who was this god?"

"Apollo."

"Is this his child?"

"This is another."

"Well, that must have been scary. Gods don't know how people feel. A god could hurt you badly even if he didn't mean to. Did Apollo hurt you?"

"Yes. Badly," she admits. "Were your goddesses beautiful?"

"Indeed. One of them looked like you."

"Like me!" she's caught by surprise. Is this shepherd boy flirting with her?

He continues, "Grey-eyed and tall like a statue of Athena."

"So, you saw Athena, and you think she looks like me?"

"You could be sisters."

"And the others?"

"Hera and Aphrodite."

"Did they tell you their names?" She plays along with him, wondering where his story will lead.

"After I chose, they told me who they were."

"After you chose what?"

"They wanted me to judge a contest to decide who among them was the most beautiful."

"So three goddesses asked a shepherd boy to judge their beauty?"

"Yes. Isn't that the most amazing luck?"

"You mean you were lucky to see goddesses face-to-face?"

"No. Lucky because of what I'll get in return."

"So who did you choose?" she insists.

"Aphrodite."

"Why not Athena?"

"If I chose her, she promised to make me smart and give me knowledge. She would change me. I wouldn't recognize myself — how I thought and what I said. She scared me."

"And Hera?"

"She promised power. I could be king of everything. But why should I want power? I'd worry that if I made the wrong choices, people would suffer. Besides, both Athena and Hera looked down on me like I was a nobody. They were impatient and arrogant. Aphrodite was short, shy, innocent. She approached me with lowered eyes, took my hand in hers, and promised to give me, as my wife, the most beautiful woman in the world."

"And that didn't scare you?"

"Aphrodite promised this woman would be gentle and approachable, not haughty and regal. Her love would be unconditional, like a mother's love."

"And does this woman have a name?"

"Helen."

"I've heard of a Helen who people say is beautiful."

"You see, the goddess didn't lie to me."

"Are you sure?"

"Of course I'm sure. But please tell me all you know about Helen."

"Your Helen must be someone else."

"Why do you say that?"

"Helen of Sparta was raped when she was little more than a girl."

"No matter."

"Do you mean that?"

"Of course. She is what she does, not what's done to her."

"But there's another problem."

"What's that?"

"She's married, very married. Her husband is the king of Sparta."

"That won't matter. Aphrodite promised her to me. A bargain is a bargain."

"But what if Helen doesn't want you? What if she'd rather stay with her husband?"

"Then, with the help of Aphrodite, I'll steal her and make her love me."

Cassandra is dumbfounded by the boy's confidence.

He sits down beside her, takes off his sandals and dangles his feet in the pool.

Seeing their reflections, side-by-side, Cassandra remembers the story of her mother's dream.

"What's your name?" she asks.

"Paris."

"Not Alexander?"

"No. Paris. I've always been Paris. That's the name my father gave me."

"And who is your father?"

"Agelaus, chief herdsman of King Priam."

"And your mother?"

"I never knew my mother."

"Then take me to Agelaus, Alexander."

"Alexander?"

"Yes, brother. You are the long-lost son of Priam."

Chapter Ten — Paris Discovers His Self

In the room Paris is assigned, a sheet of polished bronze, as tall as he is, hangs on the wall. He sees himself reflected full length.

This is how others see me, he thinks.

I never heard the name *Helen* before. I couldn't have come up with that on my own. Someone must have told me. The goddess was real. And now I know there's a woman named Helen who people say is the most beautiful. Helen is real. The promise is real. And the promise of a goddess is as good as fate.

He stands tall, shoulders held back, head high — the way a prince should look, the way he wants Helen to see him.

It's impossible for a mere shepherd to win such a woman, he admits to himself. But the impossible just happened. A shepherd became a prince. That was fate. This, too, is fate. Whatever I look like, whatever I say or do, this will happen.

He stands even taller and strides with confidence, from one side of the room to the other, watching himself in the mirror.

I'm not like other men. I can do no wrong.

Over the following days, he notices that his new-found brothers and sisters talk and act very differently than he does.

His sisters use cosmetics, doing their hair in eye-catching but difficult styles, changing the color and cut of their clothes. They want to be seen and judged.

He sees them with and without makeup. It takes skill to look so natural, to act and speak as if they don't care what others think of them.

In the market square, a mime tells stories and entertains with gestures, not words.

A bard controls his facial expressions and his tone of voice to capture the attention of his audience.

He realizes that his own look isn't fixed. He can control it.

In front of the mirror, he practices, imagining what others would think of him in this stance or that.

He strives to look more regal, yet natural, as if he were a prince since birth. He lingers in the throne room, to observe, listen, and learn.

He realizes his parents were shaken to discover he's alive. They meant for him to die. Their guilt gives him an advantage no one else enjoys. His siblings respectfully defer to their father. But he can speak his mind without restraint.

He insists on keeping the name his adoptive father gave him. "Call me *Paris*," he says, "There are many Alexanders in Troy. There's only one Paris."

Priam relents, "*Paris*? You want to be *Paris*? A peasant's name, instead of *Alexander*, the name of a prince? If that's what you want, so it shall be."

For having saved Paris and having raised him, Agelaus is richly rewarded and is welcome to live in the palace. But he prefers the view of the city, the plain, and the sea from his home on Mount Ida. He would rather hear the sounds of nature than the noises of court.

Paris adapts to his new life. He turns his deficits — his rustic ways, his peasant accent, his ignorance of what's fitting and polite — into strengths, distinguishing him from his brothers. Thanks to years of outdoor labor, he can out-run, out-wrestle, and out-ride all but Hector and Deiphobus.

At first, when he talks about Helen, his brothers laugh and pat him on the back. "That's a good joke, and you tell it with such a straight face." When he persists, they back off and stare at him as if they wonder how could anyone could be so naive?

He's tempted to downplay that story, to say it was a dream. Instead, he talks about it with even greater confidence.

Cassandra tries to dissuade him. "Brother, give up this fantasy of yours."

"Helen? Give up Helen?"

"If you feel any gratitude toward me for recognizing you and bringing you home, speak no more of goddesses and Helen."

"Gratitude? If it hadn't been you, someone else would have discovered me. That's how fate works. My union with Helen? That can happen by many different paths. But nothing can prevent it. It's fated. Helen will be mine."

When Paris requests ships and rich gifts to take with him onr a voyage to Sparta, Priam laughs. "Ships? We're not a seafaring people. We never have been. Find your mate here or in the surrounding towns. There are many fine-looking women of marriageable age. You're a prince of Troy, and you can offer any price. No father will refuse you. Forget this nonsense about a foreigner you've never met and who's already married. Besides, we have no ships."

"Then have them built. You're the king. Make it so."

"You want a ship?" Priam repeats in disbelief. "You're insisting on a ship?"

"No."

"Thank the gods you're finally listening to reason."

"I don't want *a* ship. I want a dozen — a fleet worthy of a prince, and gifts appropriate for the king of Sparta, gifts that show our respect for him and that bring honor to us in the giving."

"A dozen ships you say?"

"Yes. Extravagance befitting a prince."

"But you say your winning of Helen is fated, that it will happen no matter what?"

"So says the Goddess of Love."

"Then one ship will suffice. Why waste the trouble and expense of a dozen."

"But, father, for the honor of Troy, I must appear with pomp and a show of wealth."

"Three then. But no more. So it shall be."

Phereklos, son of Harmoides, is ordered to build those ships. He's a smith, a worker in metal, not a shipwright; but he knows how to make many things.

Chapter Eleven — Fate or Bargain?

Over the following weeks, Paris watches as the scaffolding is raised, the keels are laid, the ribs added. Another month and all three ships should be water-tight, fitted with oars, sails, and rigging — fully seaworthy. He imagines the wind, the salt-water spray, the rhythmic rocking as ship cleaves waves.

A tap on his back breaks his concentration.

"I hear you've met mother."

"Mother?"

"My mother, not yours."

"I've met so many people since I moved to the city. What's your name?"

"Aeneas, your cousin."

"And your mother?"

"Aphrodite."

"The goddess herself?"

"Of course. Can you tell me what she looks like?"

"You've never seen her?"

"Maybe when I was an infant, but not that I remember. I've seen statues of her, but they're so different from one another I doubt the sculptors ever saw her. What does she look like?"

"She's short, shy, and innocent."

"I wouldn't have imagined that. But perhaps she takes on different forms to match the expectations of those who see her."

Paris objects, "But if everyone has a different idea of beauty how can one woman be compared to another? How can anyone be considered *the most beautiful*?"

"Indeed, that's strange. But I believe it's so. I have a connection with your sister Creusa. Others might not think of her as beautiful, but to me she is. She's the one I want to spend the rest of my life with. I wouldn't be tempted by anyone else."

"If Aphrodite's your mother, why haven't you seen her? Every mother, whether woman or goddess, loves her children and wants to be with them. Or so I imagine. My mother would have, if she had known I was alive."

"And yet she consented to your death."

"That's an exception, a special circumstance. As a rule, mother-love is universal."

"Maybe time is different for gods than for us. Father says she went into labor soon after they lay together. It was quick and painless. She left me with father, then vanished, and never returned. Maybe, to her, only a few days have passed. Or maybe the emotions of gods are different from those of humans. Maybe they have different ideas of what's right and wrong. I'd never want to bargain with gods. I wouldn't trust them. As the saying goes, 'Beware of gods bearing gifts.'"

That night Paris stares long and hard at his mirror.

Perhaps Helen isn't fated. She's his reward, part of a bargain. Aphrodite made an offer. He accepted. Helen is to be his payment. But bargains, unlike fate, can be broken.

In public, he's still confident. In private, he doubts himself and doubts the deal will hold. Aphrodite may forget him. She may have never intended to keep her promise. All three goddesses may have lied.

But having pushed his father to the expense of having ships built and crews trained, he can't back down. He can't admit that he was fooled. He dreads meeting this woman. What will he say to her? What will she think of him? Will she fall in love with him? Or will Aphrodite force her to go off with him? Will they be miserable together for the rest of their lives? More likely, Aphrodite will forget him and her promise to him.

At court, Paris continues to speak with confidence, but not because he *is* confident, rather because that's the image he wants to project. He refers to Aphrodite often and insists he has faith in her and the destiny she has promised him. Unlike other mortals, he can do anything or do nothing and, either way, what matters most to him will be his. The more he doubts the truth of that, the more self-assured he sounds and acts.

Chapter Twelve — Lessons in Diplomacy

Paris can't watch the construction anymore. The sawing and hammering give him headaches. The sight of board after board being warped and fit into place nauseates him.

He hikes the trails of Mount Ida to the meadow where the goddesses appeared. Not a trace of their presence remains.

He sits by the pool where he met Cassandra and stares at his reflection in the water. That's not him. It can't be. In his bronze mirror, he looks confident, calm, and controlled, the way he wants others to see him. Here, he sees himself as helpless, confused, scared.

Cassandra appears, sits beside him, and encircles him with her arms.

"How did you know I'd be here?"

"This is where I'd go if I were desperate."

"You can tell? Does everyone know?"

"We're close, almost as close as my twin and I. What you feel, I feel. You have doubts. You're frightened. You want to back out, but think you can't."

"Father would be outraged if he knew."

"No. He expected this."

"What?"

"He has always been tempted by the sea and what lies beyond it. Your obsession with Helen prompted him to do what he has long wanted to do. He'll open friendly relations with the Greeks and trade with them. Your trip will be the start of that. He knew that, sooner or later, you'd drop your fantasy about Helen but you'd still itch to see what's beyond these shores. You're sincere and friendly, in a rustic way. You're bright and curious, easily amazed and appreciative — a perfect guest and diplomat."

"But I know nothing about diplomacy."

"Helenus will prepare you and go with you. You'll be princes out to see the world, looking for brides and spreading good will on the way."

*****

Helenus teaches Paris the rudiments of Greek but focuses on body language — how to interpret and use facial expression and gestures, as well as tone of voice. He also gives him lessons in fencing and wrestling.

"This is tangible practice at what you'll need to do as a diplomat," he explains, "interpreting and anticipating your opponent's moves and making him misinterpret yours. You need to recognize a feint as a feint at the same time as hiding yours. And the skills you need for diplomacy are similar to those you'll need for courtship. A sophisticated woman is a mistress of guile and misdirection, skilled at masking what she thinks and feels, and able to manipulate you while seeming natural. You need to learn to read and use the varieties of eye contact, to appear to be sincere when you aren't, to seem naive and vulnerable when you're aware and in control."

Part 2 — What Price Beauty

Chapter One — Leda

In Sparta, the speaker's staff passes to someone in the back of the megaron, who shouts so the king can hear. "This has gone on too long, my lord. Five years and no child. You must put this woman aside and marry another who can give us an heir."

Queen Leda coughs, then coughs again, then coughs hysterically.

King Tyndareus welcomes the distraction. He turns his full attention to her and calls, "Bring the physician. Immediately!"

Her eyes meet his. She nods to him, then collapses on the banquet table, knocking over goblets. Blood-red wine stains her tunic and cloak. She coughs more urgently and makes her body convulse as if in excruciating pain.

The king, restraining a smile of appreciation for her performance, quickly adds, "Have him bring emetics and antidotes. Someone may have poisoned the queen."

When the physician arrives, she continues to convulse. She looks scared.

Realizing she may not be faking, the king freezes, and silence spreads through the megaron. The only noise is the queen's coughing and her twitching on the table.

"Restrain her. Hold her still," the physician orders. With one hand he holds her mouth open, and with the other he pours a concoction down her throat.

*****

The queen gags. She can't breath. She loses consciousness. No, she changes consciousness.

She sees herself from on high, and not in the megaron. She's on the bank of a pond near the palace. The sunset reflecting off lily pads sprinkles her arms and legs with green. She feels at one with the pond, the grass, with all of nature.

She has never seen such color. If she were an artist, she would feel compelled to mimic it with paint on cloth or on walls, again and again.

A swan dives and lands without a splash, as if the water expects it and embraces it. Then it swims to her, unafraid, as if she were a goddess beckoning it.

She welcomes the swan, like the water welcomed it. It enters her, man-like, forceful and unstoppable, like she had hoped and imagined her husband would. She convulses in pleasure, relaxes, then finds herself once again on the banquet table.

*****

The physician wedges her mouth open, looks down her throat, reaches in, and pulls out a feather.

With a look of shock, he displays it to the king, then turns so the crowd can see it as well.

"What is it?" asks the king.

"The feather of a swan, I believe, my lord."

"What, in the name of Zeus...?"

Half-conscious, Leda clears her throat, then says softly, "Yes, Zeus, in the guise of a swan."

Inspired by that cue, the king improvises. "Zeus, yes, Zeus. He has taken the form of birds before. He was an eagle when he plucked Ganymede from the palace at Troy and took him to Olympus to be cupbearer of the gods. Zeus, yes, Zeus in the guise of a swan."

She answers, "I tried to fight him off, but what could I do against Zeus himself?"

"Hallelujah!" he exclaims, delighted that she took his cue. "Queen Leda has been blessed by the King of the Gods. We needed an heir and now we'll have one — offspring of both me and Zeus. If it's a girl, she'll become the most beautiful woman in the world, and the greatest and wealthiest rulers in Greece will contend for her hand and for the crown of Sparta. All hail to Zeus, co-father of your queen to be."

He leans down to kiss Leda on her cheek and whispers, "Brilliant! You're a genius."

*****

She keeps up the act, leaning on his shoulder as they navigate the corridors from the megaron to their bedchamber. Dare she confess to him what really happened? Does she know?

He's ready now as she has rarely seen him before. He enters her and fills her quickly.

If a god didn't make her pregnant, this will.

She wonders, can a single child have two fathers, one human and one divine? How often do the acts of gods and humans echo one another, both causing the same outcome?

*****

Nine months later, she has twin daughters, Helen and Clytemnestra. Helen is, by a few minutes, the king's eldest daughter. That means that, by Spartan rules of succession, whoever marries her will become king, even though her father is still alive.

Then, a year after that, Leda has twin sons, Pollux and Castor.

She wonders, could Tyndareus suddenly be that potent? Or did the second pregnancy come from the same coupling as the first? If a god can take the form of a swan and impregnate a woman, perhaps she got pregnant twice from a single event.

In any case, childbirth is risky. Women often die of it. And, as she learned from her midwife, having twins doubles the risk.

Enough is enough. Every night, she puts sleeping potion in Tyndareus' wine, and in the morning she praises him for his virility and acts surprised that he doesn't remember the pleasure they had together. That's her last pregnancy.

Chapter Two — Double Wedding

"Is Menelaus the best choice?" asks Leda.

"I'm sure of it," Tyndareus replies, "Red Beard has a way about him, no-nonsense, strict. She needs someone who can control her, get her to forget her fantasies."

"Are you sure? You aren't always right, you know. Getting people to believe she's a daughter of Zeus led to that ugly business with Theseus and his friend. That abduction and rape never would have happened if they hadn't thought she's the most beautiful woman in the world."

"You must admit she's lovely. Takes after you, my love."

"But *the most beautiful*? What does that even mean?"

"It means whatever people want it to mean. And people calling her that is certainly to our advantage."

"But Zeus? Was that necessary?"

"That was your inspiration, my love. Brilliant."

"All I did was swallow a swan feather as a distraction. I explained that to you. It must have stuck to my robe when I went for a walk. When that man in the back starting saying nasty things, I put it in my mouth to make me cough."

"Such a performance. Couldn't have worked out better."

"But Zeus? And gilding the feather, putting it on display time and again?"

"People love that story. It got her dozens of wealthy and powerful suitors. With the gifts and the bride price, we'll have an amazing retirement. We'll be able to travel anywhere and do anything, without the hassles and responsibilities of kingship. All thanks to you."

"And Helen."

"Yes. She's pretty enough and smart enough to play the role of *the most beautiful*. But she has a wild streak and a penchant for fantasy. I suspect the abduction affected her mind. Unlike any other woman, she insisted that she, not I, choose the man she'd marry. She believed in *true love*, whatever that is.

"Until she was ready for marriage, I indulged her fantasy and held receptions in the megaron, to put her on display. Then, when suitors swarmed, I locked her up and didn't let them see her or talk to her. Telling them I was afraid of another abduction reinforced the Zeus swan story and made them even keener to win her."

"But Red Beard? Why did you choose him? Why not his brother Agamemnon?"

"I considered Agamemnon. But he's severe, emotionless. Helen would never take to him, but she might learn to care for Red Beard."

"Yes. He's certainly better than his distant, boring brother. But yet you're giving Cly to him."

"It made sense to have the brothers draw lots, and let the gods or fate decide the winner. That way jealousy won't come between them. And, of course, I rigged it."

"You care that much more for Helen?"

"Cly can take care of herself. She's lied to us so many times and so well. I'm sure she started when she was a toddler stealing sweets. She won't let a boring husband get in her way. She'll do what she wants, when she wants, with whomever she wants, and he'll be none the wiser."

"What an awful thing to say about your daughter."

"I'm proud of her for that. Our preferential treatment of her twin didn't make her envious and mean-spirited. We had to focus on one twin as a daughter of Zeus. Only one could be *the most beautiful*. Helen has a winning look. Even as an infant, when both of them cried, we picked Helen up first. Cly didn't resent that. Since no one noticed her, she could do whatever she wanted. She's a perfect match for haughty Agamemnon. He'll have no idea what she's up to."

"You're so devious, my love."

He kisses Leda and replies, "From you, I take that as a high compliment."

She continues, "But the brothers' bids weren't that much higher than those of others. And there were handsomer, better mannered, more clever and interesting men among the suitors."

"Who would you have chosen, if you were the bride-to-be and it was up to you?"

"Odysseus. He's young, but clever and witty. The stories he made up to entertain us! He had me half believing all those adventures."

"Yes, he's a spinner of tales, a master of fantasy. But that's the last thing Helen needs. Best she be with a man's man, no nonsense, someone who will break her and control her. Besides, Odysseus doesn't want Helen. He's obsessed with my niece, Penelope. He came here to ask my help in getting her. And now, I'll certainly oblige him. He's the one who suggested the suitors swear to support Helen's husband if she's ever abducted again; otherwise, they'd have been at one another's throats. He deserves a reward for that. I'll send word to Icarius, asking him to give Penelope to Odysseus and for a bargain price. My brother can afford that. He won't be retiring. In Acarnania, you rule until you die. Such a barbaric tradition."

Chapter Three — The Handmaid's Tale

Clytemnestra meets her true love on her wedding day. He's disguised as a handmaid and is planning to kill her new husband.

Let's get this over with, she tells herself. Let's see what this pompous husband of mine can do. I'm ready to take my punishment for being a woman. The ceremony was short, but the celebration is interminable.

Drinking, arm-wrestling, joking with buddies. Every joke is about sex and loud enough for Helen and me to hear, wanting us to blush and cringe, as if we were shy and innocent. Even Helen, who we all know was raped, is treated like she's a virgin.

Agamemnon will be too drunk to care about me. I'm just another body. If he didn't need an heir, he'd just as soon do it with handmaids.

Here's a cute one, hovering near him, making eyes at him, flirting with a king on his wedding day. Cleft chin, dimples, bright green eyes. Is that his type?

She's more to my taste than he is. If I focus on her chest and hips, I can imagine she's a man.

What's that in her hand, concealed by her robe? An iron blade?

Clytemnestra reaches out and knocks the dagger to the floor. It's a reflex action, to save this intriguing woman, not her husband. In the bluster and confusion of the boisterous party, no one hears the metal clatter.

She takes the woman's hand and squeezes gently. She feels an adrenalin rush, both from the danger and from physical attraction. The handmaid squeezes back, stroking Clytemnestra's palm with her fingertips.

"Come with me," Clytemnestra whispers, then leads the handmaid through the crowd, along the winding corridors of the palace, to her private chamber.

She pushes the handmaid against the stone wall and presses against her body. That's not a woman. She grabs him and smiles. They make love standing up. Then leaning into one another's embrace, they sink to the floor and couple again.

His name is Aegisthus. He wants revenge for a series of murders in a family feud. Atreus, the father of Agamemnon and Menelaus, had a twin brother, Thyestes. Atreus killed Thyestes' sons, butchering them and serving them to their father as a meal. Later he killed Thyestes as well, taking the throne of Mycenae from him. Aegisthus is the only surviving son of Thyestes. He's the rightful king.

Clytemnestra challenges him, "So you want to kill them, just kill them? You'll never succeed at that. At most, you'll kill one before you're killed. That's meager revenge for all that was done to your family."

"I'm willing to die."

"But you could exact revenge not just once, but over and over again."

"'How?"

"'No one knows who you are. When I go with Agamemnon to Mycenae, come with me as my handmaid, my friend, my companion. You'll share my bedchamber. The children he thinks are his will be yours."

That night, acting innocent and ignorant, she asks Agamemnon if her handmaid can stay in their chamber with them. He readily agrees, aroused by the thought of having a young woman witness his pleasure. Then and thereafter, following her mother's advice, she adds sleeping potion to her husband's bedtime wine and does whatever she pleases with her true love.

Chapter Four — Arrival in Sparta

Helen misses the arrival of two young princes from Troy. She's in the garden, hiding from her three-year-old daughter, Hermione. It isn't a game, though Helen pretends it is. She doesn't want to see the child, wishes she hadn't had this child and doesn't want any more.

During the long labor, her mother, at a loss for what to say but obliged to stay at her daughter's side, mentioned that the risks of childbirth double when carrying twins, and that the likelihood of having twins goes up if they run in the family. Helen is a twin, and she has a set of twin brothers and her father forced her to marry the son of a twin. She has no death wish. She finds ways to avoid pregnancy.

When people say that Hermione is delightful, bright and beautiful, that she takes after her mother, Helen smiles politely. But she never willingly spends time with her daughter. At birth, she didn't let the baby touch her breasts, quickly handing her to a wet nurse. Now, a toddler, the child follows her mother everywhere. When Helen hides, Hermione thinks she's playing hide-and-seek and tracks her down, relentlessly, finding her in the most unlikely places. Everyone thinks Helen is a wonderful mother for playing with her daughter so much.

Helen has heard that the Trojan visitors are brothers, traveling the world in search of love-brides. She orders a handmaid to escort them to the garden and to call out when they arrive. She'll be hiding in the hedge-maze to avoid Hermione. Since Hermione, like a hunting dog, navigates by smell, not sight, Helen rubs her arms and legs with rose petals, to mask her scent,

Only one prince shows up. He avoids looking at her and seems impatient to leave. She has always been the center of attention. She doesn't know what to make of this Trojan.

"Where's your brother?" she asks.

"Please excuse him. He doesn't mean to be rude. He's a rustic and doesn't understand what's expected of him. It's no fault of his own. A dream of our mother's was misinterpreted as a prophecy, and he was abandoned to die as an infant. He was saved and raised by a shepherd, and up until a few months ago, he had no idea that he's a son of the King of Troy. His manners are rough. He speaks little Greek. He doesn't know how to conduct himself in polite company. But he's good-hearted and unselfish."

"I hear the two of you are looking for brides. But no one from Troy has ever visited here, and Sparta is far from the coast, and we have no marriageable royal women. So what really brings you here?"

"I'm embarrassed to say."

She takes his chin in her hand and turns his head so their eyes meet. He looks shocked. She smiles and orders, "Say it!"

When he tries to break away, she holds tighter, touches nose-to-nose.

"You'll never believe it," he insists.

"That's for me to decide. Tell me!"

"Paris says that when he was a shepherd, three goddesses asked him to judge who is the most beautiful among them."

"Goddesses? Which goddesses?"

"Hera, Athena, and Aphrodite."

"And why him? Why was he qualified to make such a judgment?"

"He doesn't know. But it was more a matter of bribes than of judgment. Hera offered him power, Athena wisdom, and Aphrodite the most beautiful woman in the world."

"Which did he choose?"

"The woman."

Helen laughs. "Well if Aphrodite gave him such a woman, why is he traveling the world, looking for a bride?"

"She told him that you, Helen, queen of Sparta, are the most beautiful woman in the world."

Helen blushes and smiles, raises her hands high and laughs out loud.

"Yes. You," he continues. "And he believed that dream of his as if it were divine truth. He was convinced that that was his fate."

"But didn't he know I'm married, married to a king? How could he imagine that I would be his?"

"Absurd as it sounds, that was his obsession."

She laughs again. "How flattering." She walks away a few steps, picks a rose, then turns back to ask, "*Was*? You said *was*?"

"Until we got to Salamis."

"What happened in Salamis?"

"Before we got there, he had his doubts about the goddess, but still wanted to meet you, in case the promise was real and you were the one. But he's immature. His emotions can change at the bat of an eyelash."

"Whose eyelash?"

"A young woman he saw on the dock as our ship was leaving Salamis. Their eyes met. That was all it took. We had already sent word ahead to Sparta, so we had to continue. But he wants to return to Salamis as soon as we're finished here."

"How odd," she mutters, and closes her eyes. "You're telling me that Paris thought that all he had to do was show up at my palace, and I would fall in love with him? He doesn't even know Greek, but he made a hazardous sea crossing to meet me. And he does all this because he thinks a goddess promised me to him? But she didn't say anything to me. And he had no plan for what to do about my husband. He presumed that I would give up my life as a queen, abandon my daughter, and elope with a stranger? And on his way here he made eye contact with another woman, whose name he doesn't know, and now he thinks he's in love with her?"

"I shouldn't have told you that."

"This is hilarious. I'll tell our bard. He may turn it into song."

She starts to walk away, then stops, turns back, and says, "Send Paris to me here. I'd like to talk to him."

Chapter Five — Tamer of Horses

Paris gets lost in the hedge-maze. Helenus gave him clear directions. He doesn't want to shout like a country bumpkin or a fool. When he sees her, he'll stand tall, with a haughty look; polite but distant; respectful, like a diplomat; not awkward and over-anxious, like a suitor.

He remembers his mother's words before he left Troy. "No one is making you do this. If you saw Aphrodite, she didn't give you an order. She offered you an opportunity. You can take it or leave it. Is beauty all there is to Helen? Or do you feel a deeper attraction? If it's beauty alone, what's that worth? What price beauty?"

He's cured of his obsession. Hecuba will be glad to hear that. But, of course, he's curious. He'd rather reject this woman, than be rejected by her.

After an embarrassingly long time, he spots her, sitting on a bench plucking petals from a rose bush and crushing them with her feet. She looks annoyed, impatient. She doesn't notice him, and he doesn't call attention to himself.

He thinks, this couldn't be the Helen Aphrodite promised. She looks ordinary; pleasing, but not special. For this, I came so far? For this, I left behind the Fair Maid of Salamis, with her sparkling eyes and her magical connection with me? Rumor doesn't a beauty make.

She spots him, then says something he doesn't understand. He's not as good at languages as he had hoped. He settles awkwardly on a bench facing her and answers haltingly, in Greek, "Please speak slowly. I begin to learn Greek."

"I'm speaking your language, not mine."

"What?"

"Of course I speak Luwian. What would you expect of a queen?"

"And what did you ask?"

"Did Aphrodite tell you I would be yours?"

"So I thought," he admits, avoiding eye contact. "She said *Helen*, but didn't say *Helen of Sparta*. Just *Helen*. When I heard of your reputation, I presumed you must be the one. I made a mistake. I shouldn't be here. I shouldn't long for another man's wife."

"Do you long for me?"

"No. Not now. But I did. One day I was a shepherd, and the next I was the son of the king. I thought I'd keep being lucky, like a gambler who wins once and thinks he'll keep winning. I apologize to you for my arrogance, expecting you to fall in love with me and run off with me, a total stranger."

"And now you no longer believe in your goddess and her promise?"

"That was a dream. My sister Cassandra believes she was raped by Apollo and that he gave her the gift of knowing the future. Madness may run in my family. Now I suspect there was no goddess, no beauty contest. Maybe there are no gods at all."

"Am I such a disappointment?"

He looks at her directly and hesitates. Most men would take that question as a cue and compliment her. Paris stares awkwardly. He's unimpressed by her and can't think of anything to say.

Finally, she breaks the silence, "Maybe there are gods, and there is a goddess of love, and maybe you saw her. Maybe she promised you *Helen*; but meant someone else with that name. Maybe that's the name of the girl you saw on the dock at Salamis."

"My brother told you?"

"Yes. You should go back and find her. Maybe the promise of a goddess is a half-way thing. You're given a chance, but you have to grab it. You have to take risks to prove you're worthy of the gift. There you were — a shepherd turned prince, travelling the world in search of your true love. But when you found her, you did nothing to win her. You should have insisted the captain turn the ship around. Or you should have jumped into the sea and swum to her. That's what I would have done."

"Can you swim?"

"No. But that wouldn't stop me. Nothing would stop me if I thought I was in love. Where's your gumption? Where's your sense of romance? Where's your daring?"

"If I had my horse here, I'd show you daring."

"You race chariots?"

"No. I ride horses."

"Horses aren't for riding. There's no way to control a horse. You might stay mounted for a while, but at the first stumble or the first fright, the horse would throw you."

"It's not easy, but it can be done. It takes skill to sit astride the bare back of a galloping horse, to balance, to become one with the horse, moving with it as it moves."

"And you can do that?"

"Agelaus, the shepherd who raised me, is a Scythian. He has deep knowledge of horses. He can ride bareback, with his hands free so he can hold and shoot a bow at full gallop."

"Impossible."

Paris laughs. "I, too, can do that."

"Show me," she insists.

"My horse, Boreas — swift as the north wind — is home at Troy."

"I've heard that Trojans are *tamers of horses,* but I've never heard that they could do tricks like that. In Sparta, horses pull wagons and chariots and ploughs. If you can ride a horse astride, sitting upright, not just tied to the horse's back, show me. And if you need to train a horse first, then do that. Please."

"That would take time."

"How much time would it take for a *tamer of horses* to do that?"

"To just ride, not to do tricks like shooting arrows or leaning over the side of a galloping horse to touch my hands to the ground?"

"How long?"

"A week, maybe two."

"Then do it. I dare you."

"My brother and I aren't planning to stay here that long."

"Menelaus will be leaving soon for Crete. He has business there that can't wait. He plans to hold a banquet in your honor on his return. It would be a breach of courtesy for you to leave before that. Talk to his charioteer and pick a horse that's quick to learn. I want to see you ride a horse. Better still, I want you to teach me to ride as well."

Paris laughs.

She continues, "So it's a joke? You were teasing me? People can't ride horses like that, just as there's no such thing as a centaur."

He laughs still louder.

"Are you telling me that centaurs are real?" she asks. "Have you seen one? Have you ridden one?"

"No. That's not what's funny."

"Then what is?"

"The image of you on horseback."

"You don't think I'm capable of that? You think women can't do what men can?"

"No. It's a matter that isn't to be discussed in polite company, or so I've been told these last few months."

"And what's that?"

"Women aren't meant to sit astride horses, with their nether parts pressing against the horse's back."

"You mean it isn't proper, isn't ladylike for a woman to be seen doing that? Propriety be damned. I'm a queen. I do what I want. Besides, no one need know. I dare you to teach me."

"Your passion for knowledge and your daring are admirable. But the issue is a physical matter, the consequences of the friction, the rubbing of your tender parts and the rhythmic motion of the horse."

"You mean I could be injured, that there would be pain? I would put padding between myself and the horse. Surely if Scythian men ride horses, Scythian women must too, or this whole tale of yours is a myth."

"It's not a myth. Men can ride, and women can as well; but not ladies."

"Because we're dainty and afraid of discomfort or pain?"

"Pain isn't the issue. It's pleasure."

"Pleasure?"

"Indeed. That's the joke. Among my people, the people of the mountain where I was raised, randy young men try to get women to ride horseback, because of the effect the rubbing has on them."

"Effect?"

"Putting them in the mood."

"The mood?

He laughs again. "Warming them up, getting them ready so we can have our way with them."

"You seduce women by getting them to ride horseback?"

"Of course."

"And you've done that? You've bedded women that way? And not just slaves you could order? Respectable innocent women? What kind of man are you? How many women have you had on your Mount Ida?"

"One. Oenone's her name. We had much fun together before I was found and became a prince. That started with me teaching her to ride Boreas."

"So you're a master of rowdy stories, and you lie with great aplomb."

"I would never lie to you, my lady." He bows to her with an exaggerated sweep of his hand.

*****

Helen hesitates. She isn't sure she heard that right. Did he say "lie to" or "lie with" or did he say the one and mean the other? "Then do it," she says, with more enthusiasm than she deems appropriate. "Pick one of our chariot horses. Train it to be ridden. Then teach me to ride!"

"As you wish." Paris smiles provocatively.

Hermione suddenly appears, races to her mother, and wraps her arms around her mother's legs. "Got you! But that was too easy. You talked, Mommy. I could hear you from far off. And who are you, sir? Can you really ride on a horse's back? Teach me, too. I like riding dogs, big dogs. But horses must be even better — the speed, the wind. Zeus turned himself into a bull and a swan, never a horse. If I were Zeus, I'd make myself into a horse. But I'm me. I just want to ride a horse, the fastest in the world. Zeus is Mommy's daddy, her real daddy. Everybody says so. But she never asks him to do things for me. Mommy, please tell this man to teach me to ride a horse."

"Only if you're good."

"But I am good. Everybody says so."

"You have to be even better for such a treat. Paris here needs to train a horse and teach me to ride. Then he can teach you. But Daddy might not want us to do that. So keep this a secret. That's a new game for you — knowing things without telling anybody. Start now. Repeat after me: *people can't ride horses*."

Chapter Six — The Right Touch

Paris asks a stableboy for help in picking a chariot horse that's smart and obedient. He harnesses it to a chariot, brushes its back, speaks to it softly, and feeds it apples and sweets. Then he improvises. He has never trained a domesticated horse, only wild ones.

He ties sacks of grain, about his own weight, to the horse's back and leads it to the race track, where he has it go around several times, gradually increasing speed, so it can adjust its stride to the extra weight. Then he detaches the horse from the chariot, but keeps the harness and yoke in place. It's familiar with those and associates them with humans and obedience.

The next morning, Paris removes the weights and, from a fishing net, fashions a rope contraption which he wraps around the horse's midsection and attaches to the harness. This gives him footing for mounting and dismounting and will enable him to lean over the side for gymnastic tricks. Finally, he rides the horse, advancing from walk to trot to canter to gallop, signaling the pace with legs and hands and words, and rewarding the horse with treats for getting it right. This horse learns far faster than he expected.

Then he rides the horse to the palace garden, where he sees Helen resting, alone.

She's shocked. "How did you train it so fast?"

"Magic, my lady," he replies.

"Wait here," she orders. A few minutes later she returns with her hips wrapped in thick layers of cloth padding. "Teach me. Teach me now," she insists.

First he has her talk to the horse and brush its back. Then he loads it with sacks of grain and mounts it himself, so it gets used to carrying a double load. Finally, he removes the weights, helps Helen to mount, and mounts behind her.

She talks softly to the horse, holds tightly to the harness and net, and with her free hand pats it gently on the neck. When both she and the horse seem comfortable, Paris urges the horse forward at a slow walk, then gradually speeds it up. After a few circuits of the garden, Helen asks to stop. Paris helps her down. She removes her padding. He helps her up again and mounts again.

With her groin pressed against the horse's neck, and Paris pressed against her backside, she feels sensations she never experienced before. As the horse increases its pace, the pressure becomes rhythmic and pleasurable.

"Faster," she whispers.

"As you wish."

He wraps his arms around her waist as he urges the horse with his heels.

When they dismount, back at the garden, she admits, "I'm panting, but not from exertion. I feel like a different self."

Paris explains, "It's the pressure, the rubbing between the legs, the rhythmic contact down there, like when you touch yourself. The friction."

"What do you mean? Why would I touch myself?"

"Surely you know. Your mother must have told you. Or you should have learned on your own. You're no virgin. You've had a child. You've been married for four years. Surely your husband showed you."

"We've never talked of such matters. Why should we? Sex is for men, not women. It's something a woman endures, forced on her by men. That's the way it was when I was raped as a child. And it wasn't much different with my husband."

"Wasn't?

"It's complicated."

"Tell me," he urges her, rubbing her back with one hand and her feet with the other.

Enjoying the contact, she tries to explain. "Of course, I had no choice of mate; that was my father's business. Then I was my husband's property to do with as he pleased, which he did all too often. I was soon with child. My labor was difficult and dangerous. The baby was in the wrong position. Mother brought in one midwife after another until the last was able, with pushing and massaging, to turn the baby around. I felt trapped. I wasn't ready to be a mother. This wasn't the life I had dreamed of as a child. I didn't want to be a mother. I passed the baby to a wet nurse. I saw her only when I couldn't avoid her. Now she's a toddler and she's after me all the time.

"During the ordeal of childbirth, Mother tried to distract me with tales of her own labors. She had had two sets of twins — me and Cly, then Castor and Pollux. Having twins is rare and dangerous. For her to have survived having two sets was extraordinary. That alone could have led to speculation that the father was no mere mortal.

"Mother said she regretted that she didn't plead with Father to find a different match for me. Since I am a twin and Mother had two sets of twins and Menelaus is the son of a twin, the odds were great that I would have twins. Then the labor would be far more painful, and I would probably die. She warned me not to have more children with Menelaus.

"I asked her how I could avoid that. I'm subject to the will of my husband. And there's no sure way to prevent pregnancy. If the priests are right, even goddesses can't do that, even the Goddess of Love. She told me to put sleeping potion in Menelaus' wine when he comes to bed, and, in the morning, praise him for his virility and act surprised that he doesn't remember. That's what she did with Father, after her second set of twins. I have another method that's more reliable."

"And what is that?"

"I richly reward his concubines when they lure him to their beds instead of mine. And when he's in the mood for me, rather than them, in the dark, I have my handmaid take my place and satisfy him. When he's finished his business, I climb back into bed and my handmaid goes away."

Paris chuckles. "And you've been doing that for years? And he's never suspected?"

"He's so used to doing it with her that if he did it with me, he'd think I was an impostor."

*****

That night, Menelaus chooses to bed one of his concubines, so Helen and her handmaid have the room to themselves, and Helen indulges her curiosity. She experiments, stroking herself with fingers, with cloth, and with objects. That feels good. But the more she touches, the more she needs to — harder and faster. She feels tense with expectation, needing something more to trigger a release, and not able to bring it on.

She asks her handmaid to join her under the covers. "Do you touch yourself in your private places, for the pleasure of it?" she dares to ask.

"Of course. Doesn't everyone? It's not something you talk about. You just do it. It's no one else's business, but it's natural; it's necessary."

"Touch me that way."

"What?"

"That's an order."

Soon she's shaking and quivering, with a loss of control and a release of tension. It feels good, very good. Then she helps her handmaid arrive at that same peak of pleasure.

She learns two lessons that night: sex can be pleasurable for a woman, and a woman doesn't need to depend on a man for that — she can do it for herself or with another woman, if she likes.

Chapter Seven — A Time to Remember

The next morning Paris and Helen go riding again. Then lying side-by-side in a meadow, Helen tells him about her experiments with herself and with her handmaid, and she asks him if he, too, can give himself pleasure.

"Yes," he replies with aplomb, delighted that she's willing to talk to him of such matters.

"You mean sex is that simple?" she asks. "You don't need a woman? You don't need to enter a woman, and risk giving her a child?"

"Yes. But it's far better when it's not your own hand doing it. The element of surprise. And I imagine it would be still better if you cared for the person you did it with."

"You've never experienced that?"

"Nor have you, from what you've said."

"But my sister, Cly, has."

"The one who married Menelaus' brother? Did she win the marriage lottery and wed a man she loves?"

"She found her true love and sleeps with him every night. But he isn't her husband."

"Then who is he?"

"Her handmaid."

"A woman?"

"Her husband thinks so. They met on her wedding day, which was my wedding day, too. He was disguised as a handmaid and was planning to kill both Agamemnon and Menelaus. His name is Aegisthus. He's the rightful king of Mycenae. He wanted revenge for the deaths of his father and brothers. Instead, she convinced him to go to Mycenae with her, disguised as her handmaid. He shares her sleeping chamber. She follows our mother's advice and uses a potion to avoid her husband's attentions. She and her lover make love whenever they want, and the children she bears are his."

"Whether that's true or not, it's an amazing story," says Paris. "You have spirit and imagination."

"What?"

"You dare do what you want to do and say what you think."

"It's extraordinary that you say that of me. Men always compliment my looks. No one says anything about my mind, about how I think or speak. I'm just an object to look at — a living statue, but a statue nonetheless — to be admired for my face and body. Would you like me to recite my poetry? To sing my songs?"

"You compose poetry and songs?"

"Not yet," she laughs. "But you make me think I can and should. I've had such ideas waking in the middle of the night. But it's hard to remember anything long and complex. I can't imagine how bards memorize long poems for performance — not just how they create them, but how they can tell the same story many times. Often I can't even remember what I want to buy at the market."

"My sister Cassandra — the one with the gift of seeing the future — her problem is the opposite. She can't forget. The vision she once had from Apollo won't go away."

"Well, maybe that's what bards have, or the best of them. Gods or muses give them visions that they can't forget. But remembering words shouldn't depend on divine intervention. I've seen Phoenician merchants make marks on wood or wax to keep track of inventory and transactions. And other people can understand those marks, like hearing unspoken thoughts, or hearing today what was said yesterday. They call the making of such marks *writing* and the understanding of them *reading*."

"Well, why don't you learn writing from them?" suggests Paris. "Surely you could pay Phoenicians to teach you."

"I know the sounds those marks stand for, but not the Phoenician words. It would take years for me to learn Phoenician. But maybe I could use those marks to make Greek words."

"Show me."

She picks up a stick and makes scratches on the ground, two lines of marks.

She explains, "The first line stands for sounds of Greek and the second for sounds of Luwian. And they both mean the same thing."

"And what is that?"

"I love you." She hesitates for a moment, then adds. "And I do. I love that mind of yours and what it does to mine."

He pauses, self-conscious, not knowing what she expects of him. He's flattered and doesn't want to undo her opinion of him. Should he say he loves her too, even though he doesn't? He couldn't — not so fast. But the young woman in Salamis caught his attention immediately. How could he have been so young and naive just a few days ago? What should a man say to a woman when she says she loves him? Saying nothing at all would be an insult, but echoing her words would sound false. He knows he's taking too long to reply.

*****

Helen sees his confusion. She's pleased that he doesn't feel compelled to say he loves her, without meaning it.

She says, "This is a life-changing moment."

Once again, he's speechless.

She adds, "We should run off together."

He flinches, as if she slapped him in the face.

She smiles at his reaction, that he doesn't know how to mask his thoughts and feelings.

Finally, he asks, "To Troy?"

"No," she replies. "To Phoenicia."

Chapter Eight — Where's My Wife?

When Menelaus returns from Crete, Helen isn't in the garden, the megaron, her chamber or anywhere else she frequents.

He asks Hermione. "Where's your mother?"

"I'm not supposed to say."

"What?"

"That's the game. I have to keep the secret."

"What secret?"

"It wouldn't be a secret if I told you, and then I wouldn't get my reward."

"What reward?"

"Horseback riding. He'll teach me how."

"Who will teach you?"

"The Trojan prince, Paris. Now that I've told you, you have to keep the secret. You're the one, now, like playing tag. If you keep the secret, Mommy won't know I told, and Paris will teach me, and I'll ask him to teach you too."

"Teach me what?"

"How to ride on the back of a horse."

"But that can't be done."

"He can do it. I saw him. And he taught Mommy. She was riding when they left.

"Left?"

"Yes. She rode on one horse and other horses pulled the wagons."

"What was in the wagons?"

"Pretty things. Gold things."

"And where were they taking them?"

"They said they're going to hide them. You can play hide-and-seek with things as well as people. But don't tell them I told you, please. Paris is good at all kinds of hide-and-seek, and Mommy, too, when they play as a team. I would never have expected to find them in bed together, under the covers. Mommy never goes to bed in the afternoon. But I'm not supposed to say that either. I'm not good at the game of secrets."

"When did they leave?"

"The night before last. I watched them from the garden. It was a full moon. Their shadows got smaller and smaller until they weren't there at all. But they were only pretending to leave. It was part of the game. They'll be back soon, and Paris will teach me to ride horses, like he taught Mommy. I wish you hadn't made me tell you, Daddy. The telling changes things. Now I'm not sure what is and what isn't. I don't like the game of secrets, Daddy."

"Did the other Trojan leave with them?"

"I'm not supposed to tell him either."

Menelaus goes straight to his treasure room. The lock is broken. He summons guards and has them break the door down. The room is half empty. Gold, iron, bronze, jewelry — all forms of portable wealth — are missing. What remains is scattered on the floor.

"Robbery!" Menelaus bellows.

He finds Helenus, unconcerned, eating in the megaron. "My daughter tells me you don't know where they're going."

"Who?"

"Your brother and my wife."

"They left?"

"My wife is missing. Your brother is missing. And half my treasury is missing."

"That's impossible. Paris wouldn't do such a thing. And he wouldn't leave without me. He couldn't go anywhere without me. I'm his guide and interpreter, as well as his brother. He doesn't speak Greek, nor do the servants we brought with us."

"Helen does. This may have been her doing."

"But the two of them showed no interest in one another. Paris thought she was ordinary."

"*Ordinary*? You insult my wife at a time like this? Where are they?"

"I can't imagine. He's a naive country boy. This trip is the first time he's been anywhere but Troy."

"Enough. I accept that you are blameless. My men will escort you to your ships, presuming the ships are still where you left them. Hasten to Troy and bring them back here. If you don't return with them in a month, I'll go myself with an army. Then all of Troy will pay for this outrage."

Chapter Nine — The Return of Helenus

Cassandra can't connect with her twin. The distance is too great. But she senses he's near, he's returning.

She runs to the beach. At the horizon, she sees two posts; no, two sails, two ships.

"Where's the third ship?" she asks Helenus when he comes ashore.

"You mean he isn't here?"

"Who?"

"Paris. He took the other ship and sailed from Mycenae two days before me. The weather was fair, the winds favorable."

"He isn't here."

"But he has to be," Helenus insists.

"Why did he leave without you?"

"He has Helen."

"He kidnapped her?"

"They ran off together. I presumed they headed here. Where else could they go?"

"Maybe their ship wrecked."

"Did you see that in your vision?"

"No. Until you told me, I had no idea that Paris had Helen. I thought it was impossible."

"They're dead. I feared as much. Our ships were faulty, built with green, new-cut wood. On the way back, cracks opened in the hull. My oarsmen bailed day and night to keep pace with the leakage. Paris and Helen may not have reacted soon enough. I doubt we'll ever them again."

"So he got his wish, and he died for it."

"This is awful."

"Yes, for him to die so young and after winning the most beautiful woman in the world."

"I'm thinking of the consequences."

"What consequences?"

"War."

"Surely not. Troy can't be held accountable for the crime of an individual. Paris did what he did on his own, not as an act of state. And, from what you say, Helen was complicit. Adultery isn't a cause for war."

"But they aren't here."

"Obviously."

"Which means we can't send them back."

"Of course not."

"Menelaus will never believe that. He'll be enraged, and he'll go to war, the very war you saw in your vision."

"But Troy is far more powerful than Sparta. Menelaus wouldn't dare attack."

"I thought about that while sailing here. He won't be alone. He'll muster all of Greece."

"*Greece*? There's no such thing as *Greece*. There are dozens of states that speak the same language, but they're rivals, not allies. None of them is anywhere near as powerful as Troy, and we have numerous allies, secured by royal marriage. Menelaus has a brother who is a king. And he might convince a few neighbors and friends to join him. But that's nothing next to us."

"He'll make an appeal based on principle."

"What principle? A cuckolded husband seeking revenge?"

"Paris was his guest. This is a violation of the sacred bond between host and guest. Trade among nations depends on that principle."

"That's stretching matters."

"And Helen's treachery, her asserting her independence from her husband challenges the principle that women are the property of men."

"It's about time that was challenged."

"They stole half the royal treasury of Sparta."

"Then we'll pay them twice that much in compensation. Surely, we can afford it. And we'll make lavish sacrifices. I can see it now — hundreds of our best oxen, corralled outside the city walls, bellowing loudly, sensing their imminent doom. Their sacrifice will seal a treaty acceptable to the gods."

"There's also the oath."

"What oath?"

"Helen's father had all the suitors swear that if she were ever abducted, they would rally to support her husband and do all that's necessary to get her back."

"Helen wasn't abducted. She eloped. You said so yourself. You think they're willing to risk their fortunes and their lives to bring her back? That's nonsense."

"But what if they want war? This is an excuse for plunder, sanctioned by the gods."

Chapter Ten — Iphie

The day before Agamemnon's departure, Iphie (four-year-old Iphigenia) chances on Aegisthus in his bath. She's chasing a fawn that wandered into the palace and is running, frightened, through the halls.

Iphie bursts into the chamber where Aegisthus is bathing. He, in shock, stands up.

Seeing him naked, she exclaims, "You have a thing, that thing."

He quickly covers himself with a robe.

"You're a man," she says, "a man pretending to be a woman."

"It's a game I play," he explains. "You mustn't tell anyone or that will spoil the game."

"But Mommy knows, right?"

"Yes, Mommy knows. She's part of the game. But no one else."

"Have you seen the fawn that got into the palace? I ran after it, but it ran away, scared. I've never seen a deer up close, and I so much want to pet it."

"It didn't come in here," he says. "Deer can't open doors."

"Of course they can't. How silly of me."

As she turns to leave, he shouts, "Shut the door, please."

She does, and she doesn't mention *the game* when next they meet.

*****

Did he dream that? he wonders. No, he's sure it happened. But he doesn't tell Cly. Agamemnon is due to leave the next morning. There's no need to tell her. Once Agamemnon's gone, everything will change. Don't worry Cly over nothing.

***

As Agamemnon is boarding his ship, he tries to console Iphie. He has bonded with her and she with him. She's old enough to be her own person. He has no idea how to deal with infant Orestes or toddler Electra who has just made her first steps. Iphie talks non-stop, is curious about everything, and follows him everywhere. He even lets her join him in the megaron when he sits on his throne and dispenses justice. She sits on his lap or runs around, unchecked, and interrupts solemn proceedings with impertinent questions. The audience has swelled as news of her shenanigans has spread.

"You aren't losing me," he says. "I'll come back. I can't say for surehow long I'll be gone, but this should be a short campaign. Our army is the biggest ever — big enough to scare the Trojans into giving us whatever we want, without a fight. There's no need to fret."

"I understand," she replied. "You have grownup things to do. And don't worry about me. I'll have my other daddy to take care of me while you're gone."

"Your other daddy?"

"Mommy's friend, her good friend, her best friend. He's good at playing dress-up games. He looks so like a woman when he's all dressed up, I would never have guessed if I hadn't seen him with his clothes off. He's lots of fun."

"And Mommy knows this?"

"Of course she knows. She's part of the game. And you are too, I'm sure. I found out yesterday. So now we all know, and nobody else does. That's great fun."

The wind is up. He has to leave. He doesn't know what to believe. Is she his child or the child of another man masquerading as a woman? And his other children, are they his? No. Iphie is confused. This is some make-believe of hers. It couldn't possibly be true. He knows Iphie's love for him is real, and he can't help but love her back.

Chapter Eleven — The Doctrine of Sacrifice

The army musters, as scheduled, at Aulis, on the coast of Boeotia. But the weather doesn't cooperate. Troy is too far to reach by rowing. They need a fair wind. So they wait for weeks, and rumors spread that the gods are opposed to the expedition.

"They expect a human sacrifice," Calchas the priest tells Agamemnon.

"Who?" asked Agamemnon.

"That's for you to decide."

"I mean who expects such a sacrifice? The gods?"

"Perhaps. But your men certainly do. You're asking them to risk their lives. You need to demonstrate your total commitment to this expedition. I believe that nothing short of the sacrifice of a child of yours will be enough. Your oldest. Iphigenia."

"We don't sacrifice humans, and certainly not our own children. That's barbaric. That's unprecedented."

"This united army is unprecedented. Never before have the Greeks banded together under one leader. This will be your way to prove that this expedition is important to you and that it should be important to them as well."

"Why me? This is my brother's war."

"You're the commander. You asked for that."

"But I didn't ask for this, not my daughter, not Iphigenia."

"After five years of marriage, you have three children. Your wife is fertile. You will have more. Menelaus has only one child. It's possible he may have no others. Sacrifice of Hermione would be a far greater loss to him than Iphigenia to you."

"This is outrageous! How dare you suggest such a thing!"

Calchas smiles. "That's the spirit. That's the way you should look and sound in the presence of your men. They need to believe your sincerity and your reluctance. The greater your pain, the greater the sacrifice. That's the meaning of sacrifice. Remember your present outrage and project it for all to see. But what I'm proposing is a pretense, the semblance of sacrifice, not the reality. Your despair must be credible. Everyone must believe that you're willing to go through with this."

"What do you mean?"

"A Phoenician merchant once told me a legend he heard in Palestine — the story of Abraham and Isaac. The Hebrew god, Yahweh, ordered Abraham to sacrifice his only son, Isaac. Abraham and his wife had been childless until old age, when Isaac was born — a miracle. When Isaac was nearly a man, strong and intelligent, loving and loved, a delight to his parents, Yahweh ordered Abraham to kill him, not for having committed a crime or a sacrilege, but as proof of faith and obedience. Abraham took Isaac to an altar on a mountaintop. Both trembled with fear. As the father raised his hand to slit his son's throat, the god stopped his hand and gave him a goat to sacrifice instead. That's the kind of pantomime I want you to perform. Everyone, but you and I, must believe your willingness to do the deed. Then I'll proclaim that Artemis, the goddess who demanded the sacrifice, has relented and will accept a deer instead."

"Impossible!"

"You know and I know that what we do or don't do won't change the wind. But this army of yours, these men you expect to risk their lives for you, believe in the power of the gods and the need to pray and sacrifice to them. Much is beyond the control of man. The unknown can inspire dread — objectless, limitless fear. It's the job of priests and kings to alleviate that anxiety. Your father must have taught you that. It's your duty as king to help your people get past such doubt, to inspire confidence that the gods support them. Look strong and confident. Make them believe you're willing to make such a sacrifice for their sake, a sacrifice greater than any they would make.

"Think of this as a pageant. Go through the motions as if what you're doing is real. Everyone will be watching. Let them feel your dilemma. Make them believe that you're trapped, that you'll be guilty either of killing your child or of defying the gods. Convince them of your sincerity. Help them imagine themselves in your position and, through you, feel a connection to the gods and awe at the mysteries of birth, life, and death — the awe of religion."

Chapter Twelve — Betrothed to Achilles

Agamemnon sends word to Clytemnestra that Iphigenia is to be betrothed to Achilles. They will be married maybe ten years hence, after she has had her first period.

Clytemnestra has heard of Achilles — everyone has. He's only fifteen and has never been tested in battle. But he's reputed to be the son of a goddess and to have been trained by a wise centaur.

The messenger tells her that, for the last three years, Achilles was held on the island of Scyros, in the king's household, disguised as a girl. "That was his mother's choice," he says. "She heard a prophecy that he would die in battle, and she wanted to protect him from that fate.

"At Aulis, when we're bored and drunk and wonder when we'll finally get underway, Achilles sometimes dresses as a girl and dances in front of us for our amusement. He's good-looking and, in woman's garb, beautiful. He feels comfortable in that role. His boyhood friend, Patroclus, who joined us with the Myrmidons, sometimes puts on woman's clothes and dances with him."

Clytemnestra was delighted at her husband's choice. She tells Aegisthus, "I hear that Achilles is sensitive. He understands women and enjoys their company. He could be a loving husband. Sometimes Agamemnon surprises me. I believe he truly loves our daughter and would do anything for her happiness. That's almost enough to make me regret what we've been doing to him."

She immediately dispatches Iphigenia to Aulis.

*****

In the days before the betrothal ceremony, Iphie plays dress-up with Achilles, who doesn't know that a sacrifice is planned. Achilles makes toy equipment for her — tiny shield and helmet and wooden sword. She plays a warrior, he a helpless maiden. She rescues him from monsters.

When Achilles hears a rumor that Iphie is to be sacrificed, he confronts Agamemnon, who confides in him that this is a charade. "It's a show, a ritual, not real," he says. "But no one must suspect that. The army must believe that I'm willing to sacrifice my own daughter for the good of the cause. But, at the last moment, the priest will substitute a deer and slit its throat instead."

Chapter Thirteen — Show Time

The ceremony takes place at nighttime. Agamemnon, Calchas, and Iphigenia stand near a stone altar behind a thin curtain. A fire burning on the altar casts shadows of the participants on the curtain, for the assembled army to see. After the fake sacrifice, Achilles will join them for a real betrothal.

A deer, sacred to Artemis, is tied to a post near the altar. Iphie has never been so close to a deer before. She's delighted to pet it and talk to it and play make-believe with it. She knows that it will be killed as part of the ceremony. Calchas lets her play with the sacrificial knife. She asks, "Will it hurt her?"

Calchas answers, "The knife is very sharp. When I cut the blood vessels, to her it will be no more than a mosquito bite. She will bleed to death, quietly, gently, quickly."

"And what happens when she dies? What comes next? Does she go to the place where people go when we die? Is dying like a dress-up game? Do we trade one body for another, like changing clothes?"

"Yes. It's a game," he answers.

She waves the knife, like she waved the wooden sword when she played with Achilles. Then, she asks, "Do you do it like this?"

And, to everyone's surprise, she runs the blade across her own throat. Blood spurts.

Agamemnon hesitates, in shock, not understanding what has happened. Then he presses his mantle against the wound to stop the bleeding, as he would with a war wound, but to no avail.

How could someone so small have so much blood? She clings to him and smiles, and then she's gone.

Agamemnon bellows in grief.

Calchas tries to console him. "This is the work of Artemis. You aren't responsible."

But from the other side of the curtain, the entire army sees the shadow play and groans in anguish as well as awe, that their commander has sacrificed his own daughter for their cause.

Chapter Fourteen — Unintended Consequences

The wind changes. To Agamemnon, the change feels immediate. He has lost his sense of time, lying on the ground with Iphie's body in his arms, looking up at the stars and silently cursing the gods who let this happen, who made this happen.

His men hasten to pack their gear and to board their ships.

Menelaus wrenches Iphie's body from him and orders half a dozen warriors to take it to Mycenae for burial with the pomp and respect due to a princess. Neither he nor Agamemnon can go with them. They have to sail now, while the wind is fair.

Agamemnon rouses himself to dictate a message. The messenger is his best, with a remarkable memory. He is to say that Iphie's death was an accident. They were about to sacrifice a deer before the betrothal ceremony. Inexplicably, she grabbed the sacrificial knife and slit her own throat. The priest says that the goddess Artemis prompted her to do it, and there's nothing that anyone could have done to stop her. Agamemnon never imagined such a thing could happen. He should never have let her take hold of the knife. He feels responsible. He'll never get over this. He hopes that one day she, Clytemnestra, will forgive him.

*****

The messenger repeats those words to Clytemnestra. He does so accurately, but without conviction. Pressed by her, he admits that everyone thinks Iphigenia was sacrificed for favorable winds. The sacrifice worked. The winds changed. That's why Agamemnon himself didn't return with his daughter's body for burial. By now, he's well on his way to Troy.

Clytemnestra orders the messenger to tell Agamemnon that she understands his innocence and his grief. That's what he says when he catches up with Agamemnon at Troy.

She tells Aegisthus she doesn't believe her husband and will never forgive him.

At the funeral, Aegisthus appears beside her as a man. She introduces him as Agamemnon's first cousin, son the former king, Thyestes. He is the rightful ruler of Mycenae and her rightful mate. Agamemnon's supporters — the current generation of warriors — went with him to Troy. Those who have stayed home, too old for war, fondly remember Thyestes and welcome his son.

She tells them, "Agamemnon slaughtered my daughter at the prompting of a mad priest. I curse him. I hope he dies at Troy." The crowd cheers.

At night, Aegisthus once again dons his handmaid's garb. As grief over Iphie fades, they once again enjoy one another and grow even closer. Now they share a common dream of revenge.

Part Three — How to Make Yourself

Chapter One — Why Not Me?

"Did you see that, dear?"

"What? Sorry. Polyxena was pestering me with questions. Why is everyone laughing?"

"When they got to the point where he takes her arm in his hand and twists it, she's supposed to kneel before him, acknowledging he is now her master."

"You know I find that degrading. I insisted that we leave that out when we married."

"Of course I remember. That cost me dearly. I gave the priest a prize ox, so he'd finesse that, distracting the audience with a wave of his cloak."

"Did Hector do likewise?"

"I suggested as much. Andromache's a proud woman. He shouldn't expect submission from her, symbolic or otherwise. He laughed at me when I suggested that."

"And what just happened?"

"She got the last laugh."

"How?"

"She switched her grip, like a wrestler, and got the upper hand. She could have made him kneel to her. Everyone saw that. Instead, she made a slight bow, like a polite greeting. He took the cue and bowed back to her — no higher and no lower than she had. Then she spun him around, like a dance move, as if they had practiced this; and they embraced. The crowd loved it."

"Did they plan to do that?"

"That's what it looked like."

"No, they didn't," eight-year-old Polyxena corrects her. "I saw them at rehearsal. When they got to that point, she let go of his hand, before he could force her down. Then she coughed loudly, wildly. I thought she had a feather in her throat."

"A feather?" asked Hecuba. "How could anyone swallow a feather?"

"It happened once to me, Mother. A kitchen maid had left a feather when she plucked the chicken."

"Is that what happened to Andromache?"

"No, Mother. What Andromache did was hilarious. She faked it, and Hector took it seriously. He was all solicitous, hugging her, patting her on the back. Then she kissed him on the nose, spun him around, like just now, and led him away. The rehearsal was over with no bending of the knee. She's quite the woman."

"I wonder how she learned to do that," says Priam.

"You mean, the wrestling move?" Hecuba asks.

"She trains," says Polyxena.

"Trains?" they both ask.

"She told me that her brothers taught her how to build her strength."

"A regular Amazon she is," notes Priam.

"Scandalous," says Hecuba.

"Why not me?" asks Polyxena.

"Why not what?"

"I want to grow up to be like her. I want her to train me. She's wonderful!"

*****

That night in bed, Hecuba talks to Priam about their extraordinary day.

"You're a genius," she tells him. "No one but you would have staged such an event at such a time."

"The Greeks respect our city walls, believing they're impregnable, built by gods. A legend like that gives our men confidence and intimidates the enemy. The Greeks control the sea; we don't need it. They can't besiege us because all of Mount Ida is at our back, with unlimited water and food.

"But we're not ready for war. We've had peace for more than a generation. We and our allies have no battle experience. We need training, and not just in combat skills. Our allies speak different languages and use different signals with drum and horn. We need to learn to work together.

"So we'll stay inside our walls; and the Greeks will stay on the beach, building lodges for shelter and racks to raise their ships high so they'll be safe from tides and storms. Having come so far, they seem in no hurry to attack."

"I understand. You hope to bore them to submission."

"Yes, we may not need to raise sword against them. One day they may simply sail home again."

"I understand your tactics. But I never imagined we could celebrate Hector's wedding with the enemy camped nearby. Such audacity! And the sporting contests..."

"Yes, to inspire our warriors to take pride in their fighting skills. That Hector himself didn't compete gave his brothers a chance to shine."

"But they would have loved to have a chance to better him, with everybody watching."

"He's lucky Andromache didn't take him by surprise and throw him to the ground." Priam chuckles. "What a woman!"

"She might not need surprise. I think she could give him a fight on equal terms."

"So is it true she trained with her brothers?"

"That's what Polyxena says. I should have guessed. Her physique. No doubt there's lots of muscle under her robe."

"And she's tall, as well," adds Priam, "as tall as Hector; like us, equals. As you said before, Andromache is good breeding stock. I look forward to watching their children grow, their many children."

"Yes. But I learned something new today."

"About Andromache, no doubt. She has wit, as well as muscle."

"Yes. That move of hers was clever. But what I learned is that breeding only goes so far. You need training as well. Polyxena's reaction brought that home to me."

"You want to train Polyxena, little Polyxena, as a wrestler?"

"She's little now. She's only eight. All too soon, she'll sprout as tall as Andromache, as tall as you and I. With training, she could look like an Amazon."

"Some men like that. Hector does."

"But she wouldn't do it to please a man. She'd do it for herself. That girl has ambition. I noted that today. It's rare for a girl. I'd like to foster that, rather than have her bend the knee to tradition or to any man."

Priam laughs. "So you wish you'd done that? You'd like to trip me up and pin me?"

"Yes, that would be sweet. But today I learned that we aren't just who we're born. We're who we make ourselves."

Chapter Two — Substitution?

"Time goes so fast, my dear. Yesterday you were a little girl and now you're almost a full-grown woman."

"What do you want, Mother? You only compliment me when you want me to do something."

Hecuba smiles. "Surely, I don't need to tell you."

"Marriage? An arranged marriage? I hoped Father would relent in my case. He's made so many alliances with his other daughters. Why me? Why now?"

"Now because you're ripe and ready, dear. You're goddess-like."

"A compliment? An extravagant compliment? That means Father's choice must be horrendous. Whoever it is, I simply won't do it. Send me off to be a priestess of Artemis. That would be excuse enough to break off negotiations. I don't want to be an asset, a thing for Father to use in his bargaining. Tradition be damned."

"Such spirit. I'm so proud of you, dear. But there comes a time..."

"Not for me."

"You've shown such persistence, such determination — I've never seen a girl train as hard as you have. And now you've taken that as far as a woman can."

"You keep doing that."

"Doing what?"

"Acting like there are limits to what I can do because I'm a woman. I don't accept that."

"Well, you've reached the point when you have to set aside your fantasies and accept your role in the real world. I did when I married your father, and Andromache when she married Hector."

"So you're telling me Father has found someone comparable to Hector? An equal to me, able to accept my equality? And who is this wonder of a man? Have I met him?"

"It's not yet certain. Your father has hopes, high hopes. He wants to put an end to this war that isn't a war, that's dragged on now for eight years. And you're a important part of his plan."

"I'm a marker, a token in his game, for him to move here or there to further his aims?"

"Menelaus."

"What?"

"The king of Sparta."

"He's our worst enemy, or one of the worst. What does he have to do with me?"

"As you well know, the Greek excuse for this war is Helen, wife of Menelaus. She ran off with your brother Paris. The Greeks say he stole her. And they persist in believing or saying they believe that those two are here in Troy Your father thinks that's just an excuse, that the Greeks are here to pillage the countryside, with the supposed sanction of the gods."

"And what does that have to do with me?"

"We could pay them off to get rid of them, if plunder were all they wanted. But without Helen, Menelaus and his brother Agamemnon would lose face."

"Well, obviously, they can't have Helen. She's dead, isn't she? Their ship sank. If the Greeks won't believe that, there's nothing we can do about it. This so-called war will go on forever. Thank the gods it isn't a fighting war, at least not for us. We stay behind our walls, while the Greeks raid our allies, up and down the coast. What does that have to do with me?"

"You're so exceptional that you could be a substitute for Helen."

"What?"

"If Menelaus accepts you as his bride, he and Agamemnon can save face, accept our payment of compensation, and end the war."

"But Helen? After all this time, do they finally believe she's dead?"

"We welcomed one of the Greeks into our midst."

"You what?"

"It wasn't deliberate, not at first. He came as a spy, sometimes dressed as a beggar, sometimes as a merchant. We spotted him, watched him, without letting him know that we knew. Hector wanted to feed him false information. But your father realized we could put him to better use. He had Odysseus brought to the megaron, not as a prisoner, but as an honored guest.

"It's in everyone's interest that we end the war, and the biggest barrier to that is the question of Helen and Paris. So Father gave Odysseus free access to the city and the palace, to talk to whomever he wished, maintaining his disguise. He became convinced that Helen isn't here and never has been, and he convinced Menelaus of that. That's the starting point for the negotiation."

"So Father has been plotting this for weeks, and this is the first I've heard of it?"

"Why worry you when it might not happen?"

"But why me?"

"Father had the idea that we needed to establish that Helen isn't here. It was Odysseus who focused on you. He spotted you when you were training. Then he sought you out to see as much of you as he could."

"He stalked me? And you condoned that?"

"He thinks you're more beautiful than Helen, and that Menelaus will find you enchanting."

"So you'll deliver me to this Greek barbarian?"

"There's no deal yet, just a promising possibility."

"In other words, you want to parade me in front of Menelaus. Should I show up clothed or naked? And would he like to sample the merchandise before buying? I hear that his brother sacrificed a daughter at the start of this war. Now Father is willing to sacrifice me to end it. Will that balance the score? Then slit my throat and get it over with. Better die now than live with that, that... Spartan."

"That's good, dear. Let the anger out."

"Anger isn't a strong enough word. The woman this man married risked her life to get escape him. What an endorsement!"

"I admit I've never heard of any other noble, well-bred woman doing such a thing. I wonder what he did to her."

"So you understand?"

"Of course, I understand, dear. You're in a difficult position. But you're an extraordinary woman. I'm sure you'll get the upper hand, and put him in his place, as Helen should have."

"*Put him in his place*? As if that would be easy. I know wrestling, not how to control a man like Menelaus. Is such knowledge supposed to come by instinct? As soon as I have my period, am I supposed to know how to make men do what I want when I want, while seeming obedient and submissive? I've seen you do it with Father. How did you learn that? And why didn't you teach me?"

"If there had been time, as there normally is, between betrothal and marriage, I would have given you advice. So would Andromache and your sisters. But no one listens to such advice. You aren't listening to me now. And that's fine. You'll learn on your own, dear. We all do. All men are different, and all women as well, but the basics are the same. You'll learn his ways. You'll come to know what he means, regardless of what he says. You'll learn how to arouse him, how to heighten his pleasure, and how to delay and deny. You'll use your beauty, your youth, even your athletic ability. Above all, you'll use the emotional intelligence you were born with. You'll keep your own counsel. He'll think he rules you, but you'll be in charge."

"So that's why you put up with this male-dominated world? You fool yourself into believing that it's really you who are in charge? That's delusional, Mother. That's what they want you to believe."

"That's good, dear. Find your own way of coping, of explaining to yourself what you do and how and why. But in this matter, you have no choice. If he wants you, you'll marry him."

"Don't make me do this. I'll kill myself first. No, I'll kill him. I swear I will. In front of everyone, when you put me on display for him to judge me. A knife in the back. A spear in the gut. Or poison in his wine. I'll find a way. How will you like that? And Father? Will that bring peace?"

"Dear, fantasize whatever you like. Lash out at me, at your father, at the tradition of women submitting to men. But you will do what you must do."

Chapter Three -- On Exhibit

Polyxena enters the tent newly erected on the plain in front of the Scaean Gate. A long purple carpet runs between Greeks on the right and Trojans on the left. At the end, on a platform, stands her father. To the left is Hector. On the right, she sees Menelaus, recognizable by his red beard. The man beside him must be Agamemnon.

Cassandra, the only other unmarried daughter of the king, accompanies Polyxena on the slow solemn walk down the carpet. The event has the feel of a traditional ceremony, though nothing of this kind has happened before.

Polyxena holds Cassandra's hand and leans on her. She's tempted to do something outrageous that will make this match impossible. She could do cartwheels or handstands, exposing her body, making a farce of the proceedings. She could sprint to the platform, spit in the face of Menelaus, then run away, hide on Mount Ida, never return home.

Instead, she drags her feet, holding Cassandra back, advancing slowly. On impulse, she lurches, then lurches again, hanging onto Cassandra, as if to keep her balance. Her eyes, deliberately unfocused, wander over the Greeks to her right. She ogles them, as if drunkenly judging their looks and flirting with them, with one in particular, who dares flirt back.

When she reaches Menelaus, she lets spit dribble down her chin, and rolls her eyes like a half-wit.

Menelaus pushes back his chair and glares angrily at Priam.

Odysseus breaks out in laughter. "It's an act," he declares. "She's clever, Menelaus; and she has a mind of her own. Her mother warned me she would try something like this. You won't get her just on her father's say-so. You'll need to woo her, and that won't be easy."

She spits in his direction. Odysseus picks up an apple and throws it at her, playfully. She catches it and throws it back, hitting him squarely on the forehead. He stumbles backward, rubs off the pain, and laughs again. "You see what I mean. She's spirited and willful, and well worth your effort. She's not just a substitute for Helen. She's a better match. You'll be proud to have her as your queen. And we'll all be happy to go home at last."

Polyxena turns and sprints back down the carpet and out of the tent, knocking guards to the ground. Then she runs not through the gate into the city, but around the walls, into the forest of Mount Ida. She hikes to the far side of the mountain, to Mysia. She joins a caravan heading north and east to Colchis in the Caucasus. From there she goes north to Scythia, then east where she finds the Amazons and joins them. She becomes their queen and leads them back to Troy, where they take the Greeks by surprise, burn their ships, and kill them all.

She feels a twinge of regret for the indiscriminate slaughter. Perhaps some of the Greeks didn't deserve such a fate. Odysseus. And there was someone else among them, who dared to look at her brazenly, like he wanted her for himself.

Then she wakes up in her own bed.

*****

Walking back from the tent to their lodgings by the ships on the shore, Odysseus advises Menelaus, "Take her despite herself. You'll never have a dull moment with that one. And beauty, too, not like Helen's which fades with time. Polyxena takes after her mother, who is still striking, standing tall and proud a decade after her time of childbearing."

"No. Stop. I'll have none of her. She's not to my taste. I want peace, not war in my household, in my bed. And there'd never be a moment's peace with that one."

"Then take her sister — older but still in her prime, a beauty too, but without the drama."

"Odysseus, I was a fool to listen to you before; now, I'd be an even greater fool. You bend and stretch the truth. You would do anything for an honorable end to this business, so you can have your homecoming. You aren't my only spy. Others, more forthcoming, have told me Cassandra has brain fever."

"Had one. That's long past."

"It may come again. I don't want to wake up with a lunatic raving at me. I don't want my children to have such tainted blood. I think of Helen often now. I should have thought of her far more when she was at my side. Before she left me, I left her, ignored her, never really knew her. She was a gift from the gods. She had an aura about her, a presence that could have made me see the world in a new light, as if it were dawn whenever and wherever she appeared. And in bed, believe me, she was incomparable, giving pleasure beyond the capability of any other woman."

Richard Seltzer

"So you've had many women?"

"Enough to know the touch of a goddess."

Chapter Four -- Another Option

"Mother? Did Father send you again? Who is it this time?"

"Achilles."

"The butcher? You've heard what he did to Andromache's family?"

"I'm sure he's soft and sensitive inside."

"As if a boulder has a soft core."

"He saw you at the showing for Menelaus. He thinks you're stunning. Your Amazon look. He's never seen anyone like you."

"Am I supposed to be flattered?"

"There's more to him than you imagine. He sometimes dresses as a woman to amuse the troops. He and his friend Patroclus put on shows to break the monotony of this war that isn't a war."

"And that's supposed to make him sound attractive? He has blood on his hands, innocent blood, not just the blood of soldiers. He's Andromache's worst enemy. And you expect me to embrace him, to breed with him, to bring into the world another generation of monsters?"

"You're too quick to judge, dear. Achilles wants to get to know you."

"How considerate of him. So he wants to interview me? He'd like to know if I'll be a good housekeeper?"

"He wants to see you as you really are, to interact with you, without your knowing who he is."

"And how would he do that?"

"He'll pretend to be a woman wanting to become your handmaid and companion."

"Why are you telling me this?"

"So you'll have the advantage. You'll be in control without his knowing you are."

"Interesting," she admits.

"If you're attracted to him and he to you, do as your father wishes. If not, catch him by surprise and take him down. Humiliate this famous fighter, son of a goddess. Don't just pin him. Flip him over and press his face to the ground. Make him eat dirt. Make your father and all of Troy proud that you, a teenage girl, can wipe out the greatest of the Greeks."

"Now that might be fun."

Chapter Five — Another Handmaid

Already? thinks Polyxena. That can't be him. It's too soon. And that's clearly a woman. Same height and build as me. Trained, no doubt. Phrygian from her robe and tunic. Not from here. Mother recruited her to test me. A stupid joke.

"How dare you enter my chamber unannounced. Who sent you?"

"Your sister, Cassandra."

"That's odd. What do you want? Let's get it done with quickly. I'm expecting someone else soon."

"Cassandra said that your handmaid, Polydama, is soon to be married. I'm here hoping to take her place."

"And who are you?"

"I was Briseis from Lyrnessus. Now I'm nobody from nowhere."

"I know Lyrnessus. It's near Thebe. Have the Greeks sacked that too?"

"Yes. Achilles and his Myrmidons. They killed my husband, my brothers, my father. I hid in the rubble, else I'd be their slave now."

This couldn't be Achilles in disguise, thinks Polyxena. He'd never say that about himself, unless he's more clever than I expect.

"Achilles, yes," she says. "I've heard far too much about him. Believe it or not, Father wants me to marry him, if he'll have me. Father hopes that will prompt him to withdraw from the war. He says Achilles is so important to the Greeks that if he pulls out, the war might end. But that's nonsense. He wasn't one of Helen's suitors. He was too young for that. He didn't swear the oath. If he wanted to leave, he could leave now — for any reason, or no reason at all. He's here for plunder. You're lucky Achilles didn't find you in the wreckage. Your look is similar to my own — tall, muscular. I'm told that's Achilles' type. You could have wound up as his slave — a fate worse than death."

"So you don't want to marry him?"

Polyxena laughs. "Of course not. But in this world, what a woman wants counts for nothing."

"So you'll marry him, if he wants you?"

"I was foolish enough to tell Mother how much I loathe that man. So I'm under close watch. A dozen guards follow me wherever I go. There's no escape. Mother says Achilles wants to examine me, to decide if I'm worthy of his bed. I'm expecting him any moment now."

"Then you won't be needing a new handmaid."

"Not here. And I can't imagine that you'd want to go with me to Achilles' lodge in the Greek camp."

"Of course not."

"Well, we can talk until he gets here. I need someone to talk to now. Maybe you can help me find a path forward."

"I'll stay if you wish. I'll do what I can to help."

"The situation is extraordinary. Even I find it hard to believe. I wish you could witness it and tell the world. But you'll have to leave as soon as he arrives. He insists on seeing me alone."

"Yes, that is extraordinary. Seeing him alone. I'd expect your mother or sisters, if not your father to be here with you."

"It's far more outlandish than that. He's going to come disguised as a woman. That's his way of trying to get to know who I really am. He wants me to talk to him openly, candidly, woman-to-woman. He thinks he'll fool me when he says he wants to be my handmaid, that same position you were seeking. Strange as it may sound, at first I thought you might be he."

"Achilles as a woman?"

"Absurd, isn't it? As if I wouldn't know he's a man? You've heard the stories, right? That his mother is a goddess? Why does everybody who is anybody claim to be half god? Word is that his mother heard a prophecy that if he went to war, he'd die young. So when he was old enough to hold a sword, she hid him in the court of King Lycomedes of Scyros. She dressed him as a girl and had him pose as daughter of the king. That's where Odysseus found him and exposed his identity, and recruited him for the war against Troy.

"Honestly, I wonder about his sexuality. His mother chose a woman for him on Scyros, but he felt no affection for her. When he heard she'd died of illness, he showed no grief and didn't go back to see his son. He enjoyed cross-dressing on Scyros, and sometimes does that here to amuse his friends and for his own pleasure. I also hear that when his men sack a city, he declines to take his pick of the women, as is his right. Instead, he gives that privilege to someone else, chosen by lot. So you might have been safe from him, but have ended up the plaything of one of his men."

"So, you think he has little interest in women? And your father knows that but expects him to be so attracted to you that he'll marry you and leave the war for you? What's the sense of that?"

"Bizarre, indeed. And I'll put it to the test right away. On top of everything else, I don't want to be married to a man who doesn't want women."

"How will you know?"

"We'll be alone; so I can do what I please. He thinks that I think he's a woman; so I can forget modesty. I can let my clothing hang loosely. If I like, I can do cartwheels and handstands. I can have him massage me, draw a bath for me. I can let him see what no man has seen. If I can't arouse him, I'll let him know that I know who he is, and that he's not man enough for me. I'll humiliate him to the point that he won't want me. Yes, that's what I'll do. I should have thought of that before. Thank you."

"You're welcome, I'm sure. It's too bad I won't be able to see it. What a show. May I stay while you wait? I'd love to catch a glimpse of him on my way out. The great Achilles as a woman, as a would-be handmaid, like myself."

"Stay if you wish. I'd like to see your reaction to him."

"If you like, I could do your hair, and we could talk while we wait."

"You do hair?"

"Of course. For my cousins and friends and for myself. I find it relaxing, both to do it and to have it done for me. It helps me gather my thoughts when I'm under stress."

"I know what you mean. Not that my hair needs attention. But for the feel of it."

Briseis picks up a brush and softly, deftly untangles twists without pulling.

"Yes, like that. That's so soothing. Your fingertips on my scalp. You have a talent, dear. It's a shame you won't be my handmaid. I'd love to be pampered like this. Isn't it strange that men never learn such skills? Imagine what it would be like to have a husband who could do that? It must be a matter of choice. Being muscular doesn't preclude being gentle and sensitive. You're a case in point. You must have trained as I did to get that build of yours. Was it your father, your brothers?"

"My husband. We trained together. But training meant nothing when the Greeks descended on us."

"Your loss must be great."

"Yes. But I don't want to dwell on the past. I need to start a new life. He would have wanted me to. Let's talk about you. How did you get your training?"

"Andromache, my brother's wife. At her wedding, instead of bowing to him, as all brides do, she switched her grip, got the upper hand on him, and could have made him submit to her. Instead, she spun him around, like a dance move, and led him away. Such power! Such style! I wanted to be like her. That was eight years ago, at the start of the war. I begged her to train me and she did.

"Andromache had seven brothers, no sisters. She was the first born. Her father wanted to have a son who would become a great warrior. When her mother swelled much more than usual, her father expected a giant of a son. At birth, she was twice as large as most babies. But, to her father's dismay, she was a girl. He named her *Andromache*, after a famous Amazon, and treated her as if she were a boy, as he waited for her mother to give him a son. A year later her mother had a miscarriage, and the year after that another. Andromache was four before her mother delivered the first of seven sons. Her father continued to treat her as if she were his son, training her in fighting skills. She can throw a spear as far as Hector can. Sometimes she and Hector wrestle. She told me, 'Thank the gods he's strong enough to win sometimes. I can't imagine loving a man who isn't as strong as me.' I too have dreamt of having such a man — my equal.

"Do you know Andromache? Have you met her? She's the daughter of King Eetion of Thebe. Her family, like yours, was slaughtered by Achilles and his men. Her father and all seven of her brothers. They captured her mother and held her for ransom. Father paid it. By then she was so weak from the abuse she had endured that she died in Andromache's arms. I vowed to kill Achilles for her, as revenge, though I'd certainly die in the act. But she talked me out of that. She wants the war to end before Hector falls victim. She thinks Father's plan might work. If Achilles pulls out of the war, the Greek alliance might fall apart. But if I were to kill him, they'd be inspired to avenge him."

"Would you do that?"

"Yes. I believe I would. We're all capable of many things we never do. And we never know for sure what we'll do until we do it. That Achilles is a beast; no, worse than that — he's a Greek. Briseis, please don't stop. Your fingers are magical. Please rub my neck that way, and my back, between the shoulder blades. Can you do massage as well? What a gem you are. Surely, someone here will want your services. I'll ask around. Yes, there; right there. And lower, too, please."

*****

Polyxena loses track of time. Does she fall asleep? Briseis' touch is hypnotic.

Then she notices pressure against her thigh. Not from hip or leg. Anatomically impossible, unless she's a he, unless she's Achilles himself.

She restrains herself. She needs to sort out what this means before she reveals that she knows. But he must already know that she knows.

She asks herself, How could Achilles, the legendary warrior, be so sensitive, so warm, so gentle? How could he talk about himself the way he did, unless he has regrets and wants to change? How could he have no interest in women — when he's so obviously aroused by me?

Perhaps it was wrong for me to judge him without knowing him.

Is that a tear in his eye? Is he trembling from restrained emotion? Or is that my imagination? Do I see that because I want to? The great man brought low by the sharp edge of my tongue?

He starts to pull back. Maybe he realizes that she feels his growing interest, that she knows, and knows he knows she knows. Then he moves closer, presses tighter.

She thinks, He's on the brink of embracing me, kissing me, letting our bodies talk to one another. I want him to. I'm shocked at how much I want him.

But how can I want him? I hate him! He tricked me, and I fell for it.

*****

Without thinking, acting on instinct, she reaches back and grabs his arm by the elbow. Before he realizes what she's doing, she maneuvers behind him and twists his arm.

He recovers, breaks out of her armlock, and spins around to face her. Then she slips one of her legs between his and sweeps him off his feet.

They both fall to the ground with her on top.

They squirm together on the floor. She savors the strain on her muscles as she shifts into a better position, pushing against and flowing alongside the force of the great Achilles. It's impossible to tell who's in control.

Then she manages to get behind him again, puts one arm on the back of his neck, and wraps the other around his bicep, preventing him from releasing her hold on him. And she uses that leverage to twist him, forcing his head down towards her crotch. Does he sense how aroused she is?

He counters her, gripping her arm to wrench it off. But her second hand comes down on his before he can finish. Her angle gives her the advantage. She bares her teeth, proud to have bested the great Achilles.

As he stops struggling, she eases her grip. When he turns to face her, his smile echoes hers.

Without consciously deciding to do so, she uses her hands to caress rather than restrain him. She never imagined anyone could have such muscles — so firm yet responsive, so powerful yet gentle.

She feels his hardness pressing against her hips.

He kisses her on the base of her neck, and finally (why did it take so long?) he caresses her breasts.

More. She wants more.

But instead, he stops. His hardness is no longer hard.

She rests her head on his shoulder, and he massages her back, focusing on the spot between her shoulder blades and wandering up and down.

She could love this man.

Their lips hover near one another. Their hands, arms, and legs respond to one another.

"Briseis," she whispers playfully.

He hesitates, then pulls back. A look of shock.

Why should he be surprised by the name he called himself?

He scrambles and stands and stumbles to the door.

Then he's gone, without a word.

She hopes he'll come back, that he'll want her at any price, and that Father will give her to him.

*****

His clothes are in disarray, and he has a wild look in his eyes as he races past her brothers in the corridor. They presume that she seduced him, or he her, or both one another. Odysseus says he's confident that their hopes will come to pass.

Later they hear that, on the previous day, in the division of spoils after the sack of Lyrnessus, when Achilles had his choice of women, instead of giving that choice to one of his captains, as he always had before, he kept one for himself. Her name was *Briseis*.

Part Four — About Fate

Chapter One — Sarpedon and Eurypylus

"I've found a use for you," Priam tells Cassandra.

"Agamemnon?"

"No. I'll not match you with a married man, to be his concubine."

"Shouldn't Mother have a say?"

"This is a matter of state."

"So who are you giving me to?"

"Sarpedon. He's not just a prince; he's king of Lycia. And Lycia is not just a city; it's a region with many cities and towns. I've offered you to him, and he seems ready to accept."

"Because of my legendary beauty?"

Priam chuckles. "He has reservations about you, from what he's heard about your fits, long ago. But his people clamor to join us and drive away the Greeks, rather than stand alone, easy prey."

"Why not Polyxena?"

"Menelaus just rejected her. Sarpedon doesn't want another man's leavings. Besides, she's unpredictable. She swore she loathed Achilles, and now she wants him and no one else. She's young. She'll grow out of it. But I need Lycia now. I'm counting on you to be obedient and lovable. We can't afford to botch this match."

"Is this the Sarpedon said to be a son of Zeus."

"Yes. That makes him Helen's half-brother, if you believe such tales. I hear he's tolerably handsome. But you'll marry him even if he's the ugliest, most ill-tempered man in the world."

"I don't know what to say."

"Just do what I say." He stands to hug Cassandra and send her on her way. But Eurypylus rushes into the megaron, and Priam sits back down on his throne to greet this unexpected guest. "Welcome, nephew. It's been far too long since last we saw you. Have you come with an army to help us? Is your father honoring our treaty?"

"I come to tell you what I hoped I would never have to say."

"What's that?"

"That Father will never send you aid. He has pledged to be neutral in your war with the Greeks."

"But the treaty? We expected he would come as soon as he could, that the delay was due to the threat of Greek raids on Mysia."

"You were right to expect that."

"Then why this pledge of neutrality?"

"Achilles."

"Did he sack Mysia?"

"He tried, but we survived his onslaught, at great cost. Father ..."

"He's not dead, is he?"

"No, not yet. What happened was uncanny."

"You speak in riddles."

"That's because the story makes no sense. I wouldn't have believed it if I hadn't seen it."

"Please explain. This is unlike Telephus and your mother, my dear sister. She would never sanction such a breach of trust."

"But she does. She convinced Father to make this hard decision."

"That's impossible."

"Not as impossible as what led to this."

"Please, nephew, my almost son by marriage, tell me how this came to pass."

"Achilles came with his Myrmidons. They sailed past us up the Hellespont, to the Sea of Marmora and the Black Sea. We were relieved. Perhaps we would be spared the fate of Abydos and so many of our neighbors. Perhaps Achilles was tempted by richer loot to be found farther east. We dropped our guard and prepared to send you the reinforcements we had promised. Then the Greeks appeared again, not by sea, but by land. We had dug deep trenches and built battle works to the north, facing the sea. They marched around us and attacked from the south where we had no defenses. They struck by night, breaching the south gate and swarming into the city. The battle raged all day. Then they pulled back. We had done the impossible. We had repelled Achilles' army of Myrmidons. We had survived."

"Wonderful!" exclaims Priam. "Such great news, and you delivered the story with such drama. You made me believe the worst, then revealed that you beat the best of the Greeks, giving me renewed hope that soon, with your help, we'll beat them all."

"We thought that as well, until I came upon Father in the street in front of the palace, in a pile of dead and wounded."

"Dead? Telephus killed at the moment of victory? The gods are cruel."

"More cruel than you can imagine."

"What do you mean?"

"He lives."

"Then joy again! Please spare me such deceitful telling. It's cruel to play with my expectations like that. So, he recovered, miraculously, from a dire wound."

"Miraculous indeed. But not as you would imagine. That's why I'm here with the sad news that we cannot honor our treaty."

"This is beyond belief."

"As I said, I, too, would not have believed it."

"Then why?"

"Father had a grave wound in his gut from a spear wielded by Achilles himself. The physician stopped the bleeding and stitched and bandaged the wound. But the damage was great. The physician expected he would die soon. Then our priest and seer proclaimed that Father could be healed, but only by the touch of the same spear that had wounded him, the spear of Achilles. And that had to happen soon, if at all.

"I ran after Achilles' retreating army, and, under a flag of truce, I pleaded with him to return, with his spear, and administer this cure. He agreed on condition that Mysia no longer support Troy. He returned with me to our capital. He touched father's wound with the bronze tip of the same spear that had torn open his gut. The wound healed, immediately. I saw it with my own eyes. Not even a scar remained. And Father, saved from death, ratified the promise I had made, swearing to the gods that no army of his would ever help Troy in any way. He sent me here to explain to you the reason for our perfidy."

Cassandra interrupts, beaming with joy. "That means you're not at risk. You won't die fighting at Troy, as I feared. We can marry. We can go to Mysia and live in peace and have many children."

"You still believe your Apollo prophecy?" Eurypylus asks.

"What you say makes me believe that fate isn't absolute. It can be changed, and your father by breaking the treaty has changed it. We can marry without fear that you'll die on the battlefield."

"Madness!" he exclaims and leaves.

On the way out, he passes Sarpedon and tells him, "I hear you want her. You're welcome to her. She's a raving maniac."

Priam greets him with surprise. "Welcome Sarpedon! I didn't expect you so soon." He steps in front of Cassandra to block Sarpedon's view of her. He whispers to her, "Quickly. Get hold of yourself."

Meanwhile, she has a flashback from the vision she had nine years before. She sees Sarpedon hit by a spear in the chest above the left nipple. He topples, then grovels in the dust, until the last quivering of life leaves him. And she knows who will kill him. "*Achilles who is not Achilles,*" she says aloud.

"What are you saying?" asks Sarpedon.

"You, Sarpedon, son of Zeus, will die at the hand of *Achilles who is not Achilles.*"

"What could that mean? That's nonsense. You are, indeed, a raving lunatic."

He leaves immediately, but he sends word that he agrees to alliance without marriage.

Chapter Two — Not So Happy Returns

"That?" exclaims Menelaus. "You tell me that that is Helen? You can't believe that I'm that gullible. You went to great lengths to prove to me that she's dead. You swore she died ten years ago. And now she shows up? What an insult to my intelligence. What a whiplash to my emotions.

"I'm grieving about her death, knowing that I'll never see her again, that we'll never be able to share, regret, and undo our wrongs to one another. And now you tell me she's alive? And worse than that, you point at that creature standing in the corner and claim that she's Helen? She's more male than female. She looks nothing like Helen, has none of her storied beauty, her glow, her aura. Maybe she's a peasant. Maybe you chose her at random, as a sacrifice to end the war. To have picked her as your Helen pretender is an insult."

Priam admits, "I've never seen Helen before, and this woman certainly doesn't match the image of her I had from her legend. But my son Paris says that's she. Talk to this woman yourself, and look at her more closely. Surely, you should know Helen if anyone does. Remember, it's been ten years since last you saw her. With all she's been through, it's possible she's changed. Also, your image of her may have grown in her absence. Imagination magnifies memories. You and so many others have risked so much for her that you think she's godlike and find it hard to recognize her in this frail and flawed human."

"She was like a goddess. The real Helen was the daughter of Zeus himself. She would never show herself in public like this, with close-cropped hair and a jagged scar on her cheek. You should have decked her in queen's clothes, used cosmetics, given her false hair since she has so little of her own. Why do you bring this woman before me like this?"

"I sent word to you immediately. I wanted you to see her as I did. Unadorned. Authentic."

"Authentic? Nonsense. If you want to fool me, do me the courtesy of making a better try at it. As she is, she's an insult to me and an insult to the memory of my wife."

"I understand your skepticism. I too doubted their story when I first heard it. In those ten years they've been missing, they sailed to the ends of the Earth and saw all there is to see. They were beyond the Pillars of Heracles, at the outer Ocean itself when they first heard that we are locked in war and that they are the cause of it. They want to atone for the harm they've done. They know their lives are forfeit for their crime. They don't expect forgiveness. They are surrendering themselves to you for punishment. They ask only that you end this war and go home, that innocent people be allowed to go on with their lives, in peace. Talk to them. Please. Hear their story and judge for yourself. I wouldn't bring them to you if I myself were not convinced of the truth of what they say."

Paris explains, "Our ship was made with green wood, an amateur's mistake. Cracks opened up and expanded. We hopped from one island to the next, filling the cracks with pine tar. We went to Sidon. We didn't dare go to Troy. Father would have sent us back to you under guard, with all we had taken and compensation besides. That's the kind of man he is. Of course we fled. We had no alternative.

"In Sidon, we released our crew and captain and paid them handsomely. None of them returned to Troy. Instead, they settled there and found work and built new lives, rather than risk the long voyage home and punishment for helping us.

"Helen and I bought a seaworthy ship made with wood that was properly aged. We also bought fine cloth that we could trade in other ports. We became merchants. Rather than spend our stolen wealth, we would increase it by trade. There might be no limit to how long and how far we could travel. But it wasn't as easy as we thought. Pirates were everywhere. That's how Helen got the scar you see."

"Enough, Paris, if you are Paris. Tell me no yarns of your travels. I want to hear from your lady. Tell me, woman; say something to convince me that you're Helen. Or, better still, like a goddess, cast off this human form and show yourself once again in the body I knew and loved — the stuff of legend."

"But I can't do that, Red Beard. I am as you see me — a mere mortal."

"Red Beard? You call me Red Beard? Paris must have told you that. He probably rehearsed you for this performance. Speak. And don't tell me well-known facts. Say things that only Helen and I would know."

"You didn't know me very well. You never tried to know me. Nor did I know you."

"I was your husband. We shared a bed. What could be more intimate than that?"

"After the birth of Hermione, you never had me."

"What nonsense is that?"

"When you wanted me instead of one of your concubines, in the dark my handmaid took my place. It was her you groped and entered, not me. You got used to her ways. You enjoyed her mightily, or so you told me in the morning, after she had gone. You were so proud of yourself. But I was never yours, never willingly.

"If you still want me back, knowing that, knowing that I loathe you, then I'm yours. But your crudeness, your insensitivity and my escape from that false union should be a private matter, not cause for war. Torture me, kill me if you wish. But end the war. Our private tragedy is no reason for the misery and death of others."

"No!" Paris speaks up. "I challenge you, Menelaus, to meet me one-on-one, in single combat. If I win, if I compel you to submit, you leave with all the Greeks and renounce your claim to Helen. If you win, kill me and take Helen; but the war ends then too."

"A fight to the death for Helen and for an end to the war? A fight of me against you? You, of all people, will be the champion of Troy? Have you ever held a sword, much less used one in combat? Fight me and I'll cut you slowly and painfully, lopping off this and that piece of you. Surrender without a fight, and I'll give you a quick and painless death."

"And Helen?"

"I'll do with her as I please."

"Being dead, I'll have no way to contest that. What of Troy? What becomes of Troy?"

"Troy is ours. But we'll spare your people. Leave the city to us, intact — no burning, no destruction. And in return, we'll let your people go into exile, wherever they wish, with safe passage, taking with them all they can carry."

"Better that than endless war. So combat it is. But beware. You don't know what you're up against."

"You mean the Goddess of Love? I've heard that tale of yours. You're expecting Aphrodite herself to fight at your side and save you? Believe that if you wish. And I'll believe in the sharp edge of my sword. I'll meet you at dawn tomorrow by your Scaean Gate. To the death!"

Chapter Three — Second Sight

Standing on the ramparts, waiting to watch the single combat between Paris and Menelaus, Cassandra asks her father, "Do you trust the Greeks to do as they say?"

"Why not? So much that has happened is outlandish, impossible. That Eurypylus appear just as Sarpedon was ready to marry you? That Paris and Helen are alive? That they return nine years into the war they started? That Paris die in single combat, ending the war?"

"I sense that won't happen."

"What's in doubt? In plain daylight, one-on-one, Paris is no match for Menelaus. This will be butchery, not combat. It's fated."

"Father, fate isn't what's likely. It's what happens. And I sense that that is not what happens now. For better or worse, Paris lives. He has more to do."

"Nonsense. This isn't women's business. You let your emotions sway your reason. Go to your room to pray and weave, like Helen, like your mother. Paris brought this on himself. At least he'll take his punishment like a man, and the war will end."

"He won't win, but he won't die either. And the war won't end. Not now."

"Cassandra, dear Cassandra, you're losing your wits again."

"No, I think I've found them. I don't believe in the gods anymore, not even Apollo."

"That's a blessing."

"But sometimes I see what will happen, as if I saw it before, as if it's a story I've heard told."

"You're scaring me again."

"I sense a change in the weather, like an old man with rheumatism. A mist. A fog. And Paris escapes."

"Save your fantasies to weave into tapestries."

"This is no fantasy. I know without understanding why I know. We're too quick to blame the gods when things turn out in ways we can't imagine. We need to believe the world makes sense, that effects have causes; that we are responsible for consequences. So we explain the unexplainable by saying we brought it on ourselves by offending the gods. But sometimes things happen for no reason at all or no reason we can understand."

Chapter Four — Falling in Love Again

Helen doesn't dare watch from the ramparts with the mob of spectators. The mood is celebratory. This is a way out of the war. All presume that Paris will lose and die — just punishment for his crimes. And if they see Helen now, they might tear her to pieces for her share of the guilt.

They're probably talking about what to take with them and how to pack it and how to carry it — by wagon, on donkeys, on their own backs, stuffed in their clothing — and where to go for their exile. Many will choose Lycia, which, unlike nearby towns and cities, is still untouched by Greek raids.

How could I have fallen for such a fool? wonders Helen in their chamber. How can he believe Aphrodite will save him? He's mad, totally mad, like his sister Cassandra.

She grabs a wineskin, holds it high above her head, and squeezes, sending a red stream straight into her mouth. Soon she's coughing and spitting it out. Her body has limits. Oblivion isn't easy to reach.

There's no sword in their chamber. The best she can find is the iron knife that Paris uses to shave his beard. He sharpened it on a stone for hours, as a way to cope with the dread of impending death — a sign that he doesn't believe in Aphrodite. It's sharp enough for Helen to slit her wrists with the lightest of strokes.

She lies down on the bed with the knife in hand.

She will count to a hundred and then do it — first the left wrist, then the right.

But before she counts to fifty, she falls asleep in a drunken stupor.

Then Paris is beside her, holding her, kissing her, sobbing.

In her dream — it must be a dream — he mistakes the wine stains for blood. He thinks she bled to death. He prays to Aphrodite to bring her back. If not, he'll kill himself and meet her in Hades.

Through delirious, half-closed eyes, she sees sunlight reflecting off the blade as he takes it from her hand. She opens her eyes wide. He shouts with glee.

Their lips touch and then their tongues. He licks the scar on her cheek and calls her, "My pirate queen."

She isn't dreaming.

"You won?" she asks. "The goddess did that for you?"

She hugs him tight, in relief and joy.

"Not exactly," he says.

"It was win or lose," she replies. "Clearly, you didn't lose. So you must have won."

"Not exactly. There was a mist, then a fog, a thick fog."

"Is Menelaus still alive?"

"I think so. I didn't see. One moment we were facing one another — shield in one hand, spear in the other, ten feet apart. Then a fog descended from Mount Ida, covering the plain, covering the city, covering us. I ran."

"You ran?"

"What else could I do? I couldn't see him. I couldn't see my own feet. I ran toward where the gate should be, then to the palace and here. I don't know how I found my way. The goddess must have guided me."

"Take me," she replies. "Take me now. Enter me."

"But you've always been afraid. The risks of childbirth."

"Damn the risk, Paris. I love you. I want your seed. I want to bear your child."

He starts to protest. She covers his mouth with one hand, and, with the other, she guides him where he has never been before.

Chapter Five — The Wrath of Achilles

"The single combat was aborted," Hector says. "Let's not quibble over the cause. Let's try once again to end this war."

"You propose a rematch?" asks Talthybius, herald of Agamemnon.

"No. This time I challenge your best warrior to single combat. May the fate of Troy rest on the outcome. Bring on Achilles. Same terms as before. Win or lose, may this war end here and now." He draws his sword and plants the blade in the ground with the full force of both arms.

"Not Achilles," said Talthybius.

"Why not? Surely, he's your best."

"We'll get back to you on that."

"When?"

"Soon. Wait here. We'll meet in council."

When the Greeks return, Talthybius announces, "Ajax, son of Telamon, will be our champion."

Hector is shocked. "Not Achilles? Is it the plague? We hear that an illness raged in your camp, that many took ill and died."

"Achilles isn't dead and isn't ill. But Ajax will face you."

"If Achilles isn't ready, I can wait."

Menelaus replies, "Achilles will not be our champion. We've agreed on terms. Ajax will face you."

"Something's wrong. You're hiding something. What's the truth about Achilles?"

Agamemnon speaks up. "The truth is that we don't need him."

"You're lying. And if you're lying about that, how can we trust you to keep the terms of our agreement? The offer is off. The war is on."

Chapter Six — Mistaken Identity

"It can't be true. Achilles can't be dead. I'd feel it."

"How could you?" asks Cassandra.

"You have a bond with Helenus," Polyxena replies. "You've told me so. If anything happens to him, you sense it right away. I wish I had such a bond with Achilles. No! I know I have it! I'm sure I do!"

"You can wish all you want, Polyxena. But Achilles is dead."

"He can't be. Just two days ago, Hector's spies confirmed that he pulled out of the war. Achilles and Agamemnon had a falling out, they say. But that's not the whole story. It was for me. He did as Father asked. He refused to fight. He wants me. Without Achilles, the war will end. Hector says so. Everybody says so. The Greeks are as tired of war as we are. They'll follow Achilles' lead and head home. The war is as good as over. Achilles will call for me and take me with him. You believe me, don't you, Cassandra? Let's have a double wedding."

"What do you mean? I'm not betrothed to anyone.

"You mean Father hasn't told you?"

"If he arranged another marriage for me, he won't tell me until the day of the wedding, for fear I'd mess it up. Who's the unlucky man?"

Before Polyxena can answer, Andromache joins them on the ramparts. Polyxena calls to her, "Come quickly, and tell us the news. It must be good news. I've never seen you so happy."

"Hector killed Achilles." She's carrying her baby son Astyanax.

"No! That can't be. Achilles pulled out and the war is going to end. We all know that. Don't torture me with false news."

"See for yourself. The Greeks are fleeing to their ships with Trojans at their heels. And there in the middle of the plain is Hector in his chariot, riding in circles." She holds Astyanax high so he can see his father. "Helenus just returned and told me. Hector is riding in triumph, wearing the armor of Achilles."

"No! That has to be wrong," Polyxena insists.

"On the contrary. Helenus witnessed it himself. First Achilles killed Sarpedon, then Hector killed Achilles."

"Sarpedon?" asks Cassandra.

"Yes, a son of Zeus, they say. Achilles was distracted, celebrating his victory when Hector stabbed in the stomach with a spear. There was a battle over Achilles' body. Hector got his armor, but the Greeks carried off his corpse."

"Something is wrong," says Cassandra.

"Most certainly," insists Polyxena. "Achilles isn't dead. I'd know it."

Helenus joins them.

Polyxena asks him, "Tell us, Helenus. Tell us the truth. Tell us that Achilles isn't dead."

"Achilles isn't dead."

"Then who is dead?" asks Andromache.

"At first we thought it was Achilles. Then we realized it was a friend of his, wearing his armor, pretending to be Achilles in order to inspire the troops."

"I told you so!" exclaims Polyxena.

Helenus replies, "Don't be so happy, sister. Achilles will be back soon, enraged, seeking to avenge the death of his friend."

Cassandra stays on the ramparts after the others have left. She stares off at the horizon, mumbling *Achilles who is not Achilles.*

Chapter Seven — Litany of Death

A week later, Idaeus, the Trojan herald, reports to Priam, "Hector is dead and Polydorus ..."

"Polydorus?" asks Priam.

"Yes. A spear through the chest from Achilles. He was little more than a child. He didn't have a chance. His death provoked Hector to challenge Achilles. One death led to another."

After a deep sigh, Priam replies to Idaeus, "Nine years of war and I lose two sons in a single day?"

"Three. At least three. Lycaon for certain, and perhaps more among the unidentified dead on the battlefield. Also, Achilles captured twelve Trojan nobles and says he'll sacrifice them on the grave of his friend. We don't know their names yet."

"Human sacrifice? Barbaric! They started the war with human sacrifice, and now this? The gods, if there are gods, should be disgusted with them. At least, can we ransom the bodies?"

"The bodies of Lycaon and Polydorus, but not Hector."

"No ransom for Hector? No burial for him? If we had to go to war, why couldn't it be against a civilized people?"

"Talthybius says Achilles won't give back the body of Hector, not at any price. In his anger at the death of his friend, he tied Hector's body behind his chariot. He plans to drag it to the walls of Troy for us to see."

"How was I so foolish? Achilles' withdrawal was a ruse, and we fell for it, sending our entire army beyond our walls to attack the Greeks in their encampment. Now, having lost Hector, Sarpedon, and so many others, how can we keep up the fight?"

"It wasn't a ruse," Idaeus insists. "The death of his friend enraged Achilles. His dispute with Agamemnon is over. He's fighting like a madman, with no concern for his own life."

"Then we have to kill him. Whatever it takes, we have to kill Achilles."

"He will die, Father, regardless of what you do or don't do," says Helenus.

"We all die."

"He will die here in battle with us."

"What makes you sure of that?"

"Cassandra."

"Another vision of hers? More of her madness?"

"The same vision, but more clearly seen now that events from her vision are finally unfolding."

"Nonsense. In a crisis like this, don't tell me nonsense."

"Since the war began in earnest, she's been proven right, repeatedly — not just who would die, but how."

"Then tell me how Achilles will die. I need cheering."

Andromache bursts into the megaron. "I'll tear his heart out!" she screams. "Give me a sword and spear and let me at him. I'll butcher the butcher. Truce or no truce. Fate or no fate. He's mine to kill. I'll slit his throat on the grave of that friend of his. You think he's unstoppable? You haven't seen what I can do."

Cassandra follows in her wake, trying to calm her. "Achilles will die, but not by your hand. In due time, Paris will kill him with an arrow to the heel, a poisoned arrow."

"To Hades with *due time*. To Hades with your litany of death. Let him die now!"

"What litany?" asks Priam.

Helenus explains, "Cassandra has a litany of who dies and at whose hand. She gleaned it from that vision of years ago."

"So tell me! Tell me now!"

"She foretold last week's deaths. Sarpedon was killed by Patroclus, *Achilles who is not Achilles*. Othryoneus, to whom, you had just betrothed her, was killed by Idomeneus. And today Hector, Lycaon, and Polydorus were all killed by Achilles."

"And what others does she she say will die?"

"Achilles will kill many more. Then Paris will kill him. Then Paris will be killed by Philoctetes. The list goes on and on."

"And me?" Priam asks Cassandra directly. "Did you see me? Do I die of old age? Or of illness? Or of grief?"

"You'll be killed in combat by the son of Achilles."

"Killed in combat?" Priam chuckles. "Do you hear that? An eighty-year-old man killed in combat? Deiphobus, bring me swords and spears, half for here in the megaron and half for my chamber. If I'm to be killed by the son of Achilles, he'll feel the edge of my sword first. I'll not beg for mercy. Fate or no fate, I'll go down fighting."

Chapter Eight — Priam and Achilles

"Father, come rest your head on my lap," says Polyxena.

He does so and smiles. He's proud of his accomplishment. Trusting Cassandra's prophecy that he'll die later, at the hand of the son of Achilles, he ventured alone to the Greek camp and ransomed Hector's body.

"When you were born, I had this throne built, more like a bench than a chair, with room for you to cuddle up to me as I dealt with affairs of state. But instead you gave that seat of honor to your dolls."

"That wasn't long ago in years. But it's hard to believe that little girl was me, before I became a woman, before I met Achilles."

"I understand now how you can love him. He could have held me hostage and forced the surrender of Troy. But his eyes lit up when he recognized me. He embraced me, welcomed me, and treated me with respect. In pain over the death of his friend, he sought to soften my grief. He sensed his own death is near and mine as well. Yes, he treated me as if I were his father, on a final visit."

She strokes his forehead and asks, "While you were there, did you see Achilles' woman, Briseis?"

"I believe so. There was a slave girl he caressed with his eyes, but she stayed focused on her weaving. She seemed to be grieving even more than Achilles."

"Is she with child?"

"Not from the look of her. But if she were, he might not be the father. It could be Agamemnon, despite his oaths and her testimony. Or perhaps even Patroclus. They may have shared her. I wonder if Achilles can have children."

"I've heard he has a son."

"If that were true, the boy would now be Achilles' age when he first came to Troy. He'd be here now, at his father's side. Maybe that isn't his son. A strong man can have weak seed."

"Without the hope of children, do you think he'd marry Briseis?"

"I doubt it. There'd be no point. She's his slave. Why own her as a wife as well? Besides, his mind is in another place. He thinks about the death of his friend and his own death. He even talks to the dead, to Patroclus. He believes Patroclus answers, and not just in his dreams. Several times, as we talked, he spoke as if to someone else, then begged my pardon."

"He needs love to heal."

"If he should live so long."

"But he need not fight and die."

"He presumes he must."

"But one time, ever so briefly, he wanted to leave the war for me."

"So I wished and so you believed."

"Did he mention me?"

"Yes. And from the look and manner of Briseis, that wasn't the first time he had. She bristled when he asked about you. He dismissed her. Then he asked again."

"Did he ask if I'm betrothed?"

"No. He asked about your childhood. I told him you played with dolls, but not as your sisters did. Some you gave the names of heroes, others of Amazons. They'd fight, and the Amazons would win, and the men would become their slaves. He talked of his tussle with you. He joked that he was glad there were no witnesses. If you had competed in wrestling at Patroclus' funeral games, you might have beaten everyone. He said he'd like a rematch with you."

"Did you tell him I'd welcome that?"

"No. There was no time for that. He became manic, talking fast, not giving me a chance to reply. And then he seemed to talk to the shade of Patroclus and to forget me altogether, until Idaeus fetched me. Hector's body was loaded on the wagon. It was time to go."

Chapter Nine — Amazon

Locked in her bedchamber, Polyxena dreams that Penthesilea, Queen of the Amazons, comes to Troy on a personal quest. She wants to kill Achilles for the glory of it, confident that she can best him in single combat. She's reputed to be a daughter of Ares, the God of War.

In her dream, Polyxena sends Achilles a message to meet her at the Temple of Apollo so she can warn him, in person.

There are two temples beyond the city walls, on the slopes of Mount Ida — one for Apollo and one for Athena. Both are sacred ground, neutral territory. Greeks and Trojans are supposed to be safe in either of them. There you can meet someone who, for a price, will deliver a personal message to the other side. It's rumored that lovers use the private chambers of those temples for illicit meetings and that married childless women go there to catch the seed of nameless strangers.

Achilles joins her there. He laughs when she delivers her warning. "The only woman I'd be afraid of would be you," he says. They make love.

Then she wakes with a start. She could swear she feels a distress signal from Achilles. He might be dying. But she doesn't want to know. All day long, she cowers in bed, with the covers over her head.

She hears knocking at her door. It's twilight. Helenus enters.

"Don't tell me," she says.

"You know already?"

"I know it's bad news, and I don't want to hear it."

"Yes. It's terrible."

"Achilles?"

"Yes. It was Achilles who did it."

"Did what?"

"Killed Penthesilea and all twelve of her warriors."

"Achilles?"

"Yes. Achilles battled her one-on-one from sunrise to sunset. Everyone nearby, on both sides, stopped fighting and watched. I saw and heard everything."

With a sigh of relief, Polyxena says, "I should have known better than to worry. Cassandra said Achilles would kill the Amazon queen. I should have listened to her instead of my fantasies. I imagined he was in distress, maybe wounded, maybe dead. So there's nothing new, nothing unexpected."

"Achilles thought she was you."

"What?"

"At the end, they were grappling, each with a dagger in hand. They head-butted, dislodging their helmets and he saw his opponent's face. This warrior, equal to him in strength, was a woman. Seeing his surprise, she laughed at him. He asked, 'Polyxena?' She stopped laughing, looked puzzled, and released his dagger hand. Unimpeded, that hand continued its natural course. It slit her throat. Blood spurted. He grabbed hold of her throat, not to strangle her, but to stop the bleeding. Then he stripped off his breast-plate, tore off his tunic, and pressed the cloth to the wound. They both dropped to the ground. He cradled her head in his lap. She was bleeding to death. There was nothing he could do to stop it. But she could still talk.

"I couldn't hear her words; her voice was faint. But I could hear him as he tried to comfort her. There was a mixture of grief and joy in his words. He was overjoyed that she wasn't you, but he grieved that she could have been."

Chapter Ten — Achilles Is Dead

"Achilles is dead," reports Helenus.

"You lie."

"Why should I lie?"

"That can't be true. He was coming for me. He has had enough of war and death."

"I hear that he was unarmed and that he brazenly walked up to the Scaean Gate and pounded with his fists, as if he expected we'd open up. Such arrogance! Of course, everyone on the ramparts showered him with spears and arrows."

"This can't have happened. I must be dreaming. Maybe my whole life has been a dream. I'm sleeping in some other place, some other time. When I wake I'll be in Achilles' arms in another world. Or maybe he won't be there, and I won't remember any of this. I'm going mad. He can't be dead. I refuse to believe he's dead."

"But it's true, sister," insists Helenus. "Achilles is dead, and we are in the megaron at Troy, and you are weaving near the hearth. Life goes on as always. We have joy and also grief, and not in the proportions we would choose."

"It's not fair."

"Life's not fair."

"Why not? Whoever made up this story we're acting in, this story we call life, doesn't care about our feelings, about what we want and need, about who we love and hate. Our motivations don't matter. What happens happens. It rains. It shines. It. It. It. The story of our lives is all about *it*, not us."

"Yes, the illusions, the possibilities we thought were life come to an end. With time, you'll understand and accept."

Cassandra joins in. "For me it's far worse than for you, Polyxena. I see double. Knowing what happens before it happens means I can't hope for anything else. You see possibilities and savor what might be, and believe that your decisions matter, that you shape the future and are responsible for it. For me, the future has already happened and I can't do anything about it.

"Achilles is dead. You know that now. That can't be changed. For months, you've savored other possible lives in which you loved one another and lived together and changed in response to one another. That didn't happen, but as long as you thought it could, that hope shaped how you saw everything.

"Possibilities are the richness and joy of life. When Achilles died, you lost not just him but everything that might have been if he had lived. You have no choice but to accept that now to move on, to build a new set of hopes, a new life for yourself.

"I can't see possibilities, only reality. Do you understand? I haven't been able to enjoy the fantasy of what might be. Apollo didn't give me vision. He gave me blindness. I only see a single chain of facts. This happens, then that, then that. Dead. Inalterable. It feels like I'm living someone else's story.

"I can't stand that anymore. From now on, I'll try to block out my memory of that vision. I'll try to convince myself it isn't true. I'll make up new prophecies that give me hope. I'll tell my story of what might be, not just act out the story given to me. Reality be damned. I'll see the future the way I want to see it. I'll savor my present in the light of what might be, not in the darkness of what is. I'll have my say, and you should too."

"That's madness, dear," objects Hecuba.

"But you haven't forgotten yet, have you?" Polyxena asks Cassandra.

"Not yet. Forgetting won't be easy."

"Then tell me now, please. Tell me what happens to me? Despite what you say, I want to know. When and how will I die?"

"The son of Achilles will sacrifice you on Achilles' grave. Is that what you wanted to hear? Are you glad I said it?"

Chapter Eleven — Death of Paris

Knowing that Paris is on Cassandra's death list, Helen insists that he stay inside the palace, not even go to the ramparts as a spectator. But that doesn't save him.

She, Priam, and the rest of the royal family witness his death at dinner. An arrow comes through a window. After heavy rain, the curtains had just been pulled aside to let in sunshine and fresh air. The arrow barely nicks his arm, but the tip is poisoned.

"Luck, damned luck," says Priam as Paris' body is carried off for burial. "I'll have no more talk of fate. That leads to complacency and inaction. We need to regroup. We've lost many men these last few months. But the Greeks have lost as well. Not only Achilles, but also Ajax, their second best warrior. I hear he went mad and killed himself when he failed to win a contest for the armor of Achilles. Such vanity. Achilles and Ajax were always at the forefront, inspiring the entire army. The Greeks are much weaker without them. We must stand firm and be patient. Perhaps they'll lose hope and sail away. If not, if we must go down, we'll go down fighting, not whining about the injustice of fate."

He turns to Helen, "Mourn the passing of Paris with due respect and grief. But you will marry Deiphobus and quickly. I'll not have my sons contend for you as the Greeks contended for the armor of Achilles. At a time like this, we need unity and obedience, not dissention."

"But I don't want to marry."

"Your wishes don't matter, my dear. You have nothing to say about this. Your one choice proved far too costly. It's unnatural for women to have choice. This is a matter of state. You will obey."

Then he turns to Cassandra, "You, my beloved and troublesome daughter, are betrothed again. His name is Coroebus. He's the tenth son of the king of Phrygia. He'll inherit nothing, but he's a man of character and a brave warrior. He'll pay no bride price. He'll earn you by his prowess on the battlefield.

"Also, there's news you should know. Telephus of Mysia died not long ago. Eurypylus, once your betrothed, became king. He broke the treaty his father made with the Greeks, and joined us. He arrived today with a thousand warriors. But don't worry. You won't have to see him. And you won't be troubled again by your vision of his death. He died already, at the hand of Pyrrhus, son of Achilles.

"He's here now, that son you said will kill me in combat. I'd better practice with sword and spear, so I can give him a good fight. I won't go quietly. He'll remember me. I'll be his nightmare."

Part Five — Their Last Say

Chapter One — The Trojan Horse

"It's hollow," Helen whispers to Cassandra.

"What makes you think that?"

"I heard a voice whispering — the voice of Menelaus. There are men inside that wooden horse. Let's find a log and heave it at the belly. It'll resound and everyone who hears that will know it's hollow."

"Wait. What if it is hollow?" asked Cassandra. "What if this is a ruse, and there are men inside, including Menelaus. What if they plan to come out of the horse when our warriors are drunk with celebrating or are sleeping? What if they open the gates and signal to their fleet to return?"

"The war would end?"

"Don't we want it to end?"

"Did you see that in your vision?"

Cassandra nods.

Helen hesitates, then pulls a cart near the belly of the horse, stands on the cart and knocks softly, a simple pattern that children often use as a signal to one another. From inside they hear, faintly, the beginning of the traditional reply, as if someone did so by reflex, then stopped himself.

Cassandra looks at Helen. Helen nods and steps down. Together they pull the cart away.

*****

Cassandra runs through the nearest city gate, which is open and unguarded. She races to the temple of Athena on the slopes of Mount Ida, and climbs onto the altar, clutching the feet of the statue, praying that the fall of Troy be quick and without great bloodshed. The Trojans are helpless. The Greeks could be merciful.

She hears her name — shouted and echoed. Is she delusional? She turns and sees the shadow of someone in the open doorway.

"Cassandra?" she hears again. It's a man's voice.

"Who are you?" she asks.

"Coroebus, your betrothed. I've come to save you. The Greeks are everywhere, killing everyone. Come with me. Let's flee to the wilds of Mount Ida and hide until the massacre is over and the Greeks have gone."

As he runs toward her, another figure appears behind him, races at him, sword extended, and impales him between the shoulder blades.

"Who are you?" she asks, as the newcomer strides toward her.

"I am Ajax."

"Ajax is dead."

"You mean Ajax son of Telamon. I am Ajax son of Oileus. He is Ajax the Dead. I am Ajax the Living. And you are mine."

Ajax grabs Cassandra and breaks her hold on the statue of Athena. The ceramic statue falls and shatters.

He rips off her mantle, her robe, her tunic. Then Cassandra sees his head pull back, his hair gripped by a powerful hand, a bronze blade at his throat. She recognizes Agamemnon. This scene was in her vision. It had made no sense before — Agamemnon saving her and she giving herself to him, willingly.

"Do you realize what you've done?" Agamemnon asks Ajax. "You have destroyed a statue of Athena and you are attacking a woman in Athena's sacred precinct. May the gods have mercy on you. And may their wrath at you not extend to the rest of us. Leave here now or I myself will strike you down before the gods have a chance to do so."

After Ajax leaves, chastened and confused, Cassandra makes no effort to conceal her nakedness. She clings to Agamemnon as she clung to the statue. And, as in the fantasy future she imagined for herself, her grip becomes an embrace, her body molds to his. She welcomes him, urging him to do what Ajax had sought to do by force.

He hesitates. "In the temple? That would be a sacrilege. We can't."

"But you do, we do. I've seen this."

"You're Cassandra, aren't you? The daughter of Priam who sees the future?"

"Yes. And yes. Though I thought my days of prophecy had ended."

He responds to her, and he's glad he does. He decides she will be his first choice from the spoils of Troy.

Chapter Two — Helen and Menelaus

Helen retreats to the chamber she shares with Deiphobus and crawls into bed with him, and makes love with him — not from passion, but with empathy, knowing that at long last the end of the war is near, and the two of them will be dead by morning.

She wakes — how was she able to sleep? — to shouts and screams, the clatter of weapons, the crackling of fire, the collapse of buildings. Smoke streams through the window.

Deiphobus, in full armor, stands at the ready, guarding the door.

Helen sits on a stool by the bed, numb, emotionless, certain she's about to die. She won't struggle. That would only prolong the agony.

The door crashes in, knocking Deiphobus to the ground.

He scrambles to his feet and once again assumes the ready position. Then he quickly, smoothly switches sword and shield so the sword is in his left hand.

He had shown Helen that trick. He's proud of it. On the battlefield, it served him well, catching his opponents off-guard.

Menelaus faces him without helmet, without shield, both hands on the hilt of his sword.

With a piercing war cry, Deiphobus strides forward.

Menelaus, with a single stroke, severs his head.

Helen shuts her eyes.

She expects to see a rush of images like what Cassandra saw in her vision, but instead of the future, her past — childhood, rape, marriage, childbirth, Paris.

Instead, her mind goes blank.

Darkness. Silence.

The wait is interminable.

Is she dead already?

Then she hears a thump.

In her panic, has time slowed down for her? Has it taken that long for Deiphobus' head to hit the ground?

Another delay, then she hears the crash of a body toppling over.

Warm liquid hits her arm.

She keeps her eyes shut. She doesn't want to see the blood. She doesn't want to watch as Menelaus swings his sword at her.

She hears heavy breathing. She smells sweat.

Why doesn't Menelaus get it over with?

Is he savoring his revenge?

She wakes again, with a shiver. Was she dreaming? Did none of this happen? Or is it about to happen? Or will it happen over and over again, forever? Is that her punishment in Hades?

A short while before, she and Deiphobus had gripped each other in despair and tried to blank out the sounds of death, rape, and destruction in the streets below. Before that, during their brief marriage, Deiphobus and she had been polite strangers. She made no effort to know him. He couldn't replace Paris. That was unfair of her. She should have given him a chance. People change. He could have. She could have. Now neither of them can.

When Menelaus kills her, she will forgive him and wish him well. She deserves her punishment. She will be at peace with herself and with him.

She opens her eyes.

He's standing next to the bed, sword held with both hands.

How long has he been there?

Their eyes meet. She expects anger and hatred.

Instead she sees tears and regret.

There's a touch of gray in his red beard. There's a weariness about him. He looks pensive, rather than angry. War has changed him, and age as well.

If they first met now, what would she as she is now think of him as he is now?

That's impossible to imagine. They wouldn't be who they are now if they hadn't gone through their failed marriage, her elopement with Paris and the ten years of war their breakup triggered.

She says, "I wonder what it would have been like if you and I had gotten to know one another. Could we have been friends? Might we have become lovers? We'd never seen one another when Father decided we would marry. Then you took me roughly as if I were a new-bought slave. I had no choice. I was yours to use as you pleased, a thing, not a person. I doubt you got much pleasure from it. I know I didn't.

"Then, after the birth of Hermione, I became aware of the risk, not just of childbirth but of the birth of twins. I had my handmaid take my place in bed with you, and you didn't even notice. I left you, truly left you, long before Paris.

"We were strangers then. And we're even more strangers ten years later. What would you think of me if first you saw me now, not a child bride, not a legendary beauty, but a mature woman with a jagged scar on her cheek?

"Go ahead. Do what you have to do. I'm ready for it. Kill me. Pretend that you're still enraged over what I did so long ago. Or would you prefer to wait until you have an audience so you can prove your manhood in front of them? Or perhaps you'd like to slit my throat in a temple at an altar, as a sacrifice to the gods, thanking them for your glorious victory."

"No," he says softly, taking her hand in his and kissing the cheek with the scar.

The next day, they set sail on a single ship. The rest of the Spartans head straight home.

They journey southward — world-weary strangers, who on a whim decided to run off together, shedding all responsibility, not caring where they go or what becomes of them.

When he makes the first clumsy gestures toward physical intimacy, she doesn't object. Gradually, they teach one another what they want of one another, and respond in kind.

In Sidon, they trade their war ship for a merchant ship, hire a Phoenician crew, and barter for merchandise that they can sell for a profit elsewhere, as Helen and Paris did years before. They sail to Cyrus, Egypt, Libya, Carthage. Sometimes they talk of having another child or even twins, but that never happens.

When they reach the Pillars of Heracles, they're tempted to sail north to the island rich in tin, or south along the coast of Africa, or west across the Ocean, perhaps to the Islands of the Blest. But instead, they return to Sparta, where their daughter Hermione is old enough to have children of her own.

Chapter Three — Hecuba and Odysseus

At the division of the spoils, Odysseus has fourth choice, a position of honor, after Agamemnon, Menelaus, and Pyrrhus, and before Diomedes.

Agamemnon set the rules to lessen the chance that fighting might break out among the victors. Beyond the first five, chosen by merit, the order was determined by lot. They all have had two days to inspect the human merchandise before making their selections.

Talthybius raises his staff of authority. The next in line raises the baton of choice and names or points to the woman he wants, then passes the baton to the next. If there's a delay, Talthybius will count slowly to seven, lowering and raising his staff with each count. Anyone who doesn't choose in that time will lose his chance.

When Pyrrhus passes him the baton, Odysseus hesitates.

His memories of his wife, Penelope, are dim. He was with her little more than a year before he had to leave for war. He doesn't want to spoil his long-wished-for homecoming by arriving with a concubine.

He remembers what he heard about his mother Anticleia and his father Laertes. Soon after their marriage, Laertes bought a young woman of noble birth, for a price high enough for a princess. Anticleia exploded in jealous rage and made him promise, counter to all precedent, that he would never bed that other woman. Instead, Eurycleia became Odysseus' nurse and later the nurse of his son Telemachus, and also manager of the palace staff — any post of honor, but not the king's concubine.

He doesn't want a scene like that with Penelope. He hopes they will bond again, not just in the flesh, but in like-minded-ness, as before, and as few men and women ever do.

Talthybius signals with his staff of authority.

Diomedes and all the others after him are waiting, each hoping that the woman he wants won't be taken before his turn.

Odysseus has to make his choice.

His eyes catch the eyes of Hecuba — gray, like the eyes of Athena, like those of his mother. Many of the captives are sitting or are stretched out on the ground —some trembling in fear and grief, others frozen, expressionless. Some deliberately display their legs or breasts, wanting to be wanted, hoping to make the most of their new lot. Hecuba alone stands tall. With none of the trappings, much less the power, of a queen, she is still queen.

He imagines his mother grieving for him as Hecuba surely now grieves quietly, with dignity, for her lost children and other loved ones.

His time must be up. He has thought too long. Why isn't Diomedes prodding him to speak or point, then pass the baton?

Talthybius raises his staff again and shouts "Five!"

Only five?

Hecuba smiles at him. He smiles back, and to the surprise of all, he speaks her name.

*****

In the twilight of dawn, as Odysseus' ship leaves the shore, Hecuba stands near the stern. She makes eye contact with him, nods, and turns back to look at the shore where embers still stubbornly burn in the ruins of what once was Troy.

Head held high, with dignity, she dons the crown of the queen of Troy, which Odysseus let her keep as a sign of respect. Then she steps off the ship, hitting the sea feet-first.

She goes straight down.

With a gesture and a look, Odysseus stops anyone from trying to save her.

She doesn't rise to the surface, not once.

The sea accepts her.

Chapter Four — Polyxena and Pyrrhus

"What a fine warrior you are," Polyxena taunts Pyrrhus as they walk together. "Today you killed two princes and a king. The first prince was my brother Polites, a boy your own age, with no shield, no armor, no weapons. The king was Priam, over eighty years old, who could barely lift a spear. And the crowning glory was the second prince, Astyanax, son of Hector. He was two years old. You grabbed him by his tiny feet and swung him like a wet cloth, smashing his head against the stone ramparts. Such skill! Such courage! Such bravery! Who but a brave man would choose Andromache as slave and bedmate and then bash out the brains of her son? Never turn your back on her. Don't let her prepare your food.

"Your father, Achilles, found his equal in Penthesilea, daughter of the God of War. They fought toe-to-toe for an entire day; he only bested her when a random distraction put her off her guard. Andromache, in her normal state, is the equal of that Amazon. When she's enraged, not even the God of War would tangle with her.

"When she wanted to rush into battle and wreak vengeance on Achilles, Priam could only restrain her by reminding her of her son. If she should fall victim to a stray spear or arrow, her son would be left motherless as well as fatherless. And that son she loved so well is the toddler you just bashed to death. You'll be taking her into your home? Most men would be afraid to sleep if she were anywhere nearby, much less to share a bed with her."

When they reach the funeral mound of Achilles, where Pyrrhus plans to sacrifice her, Polyxena tells him, "I loved your father and he loved me. Do you have any memory of him? Did he of you? How old were you when he left for Troy?"

She looks at him closely and reaches out to touch the fire-red hair for which he had the nickname *Pyrrhus*. "You aren't Achilles' son," she says. "You're nothing like him."

"How dare you!"

As he raises his fist, she grabs his other hand, yanks, trips him, and laughs out loud. "All hail to the mighty Pyrrhus."

He rises, draws his dagger, and advances on her.

"Why did you choose me in the division of the spoils?" she asks. "Was it because I was so highly prized? Not that you wanted me but that so may others did? As your father's heir, you were entitled to me, so you wouldn't let anyone else have me. Then seeing me, realizing my strength and that I loathe you and that I'm not constrained by fear of pain or death, you dared not bed me for fear of what I might do to you. To save face, you let it be known that the shade of your father asked for me as a sacrifice. So let it be, but not by your feeble hand."

She outmaneuvers him again, takes his dagger, and slits her own throat.

Chapter Five — Andromache and Helenus

Helenus gently removes the gag and blindfold from Andromache.

"You? Here?" she asks. "Why are you here? Why are you alive and unscarred? You were captured by the Greeks and you colluded with them. Traitor! I'd kill you now with my own hands if they weren't bound."

"I wanted to end the war. I wanted peace."

"You call that ending the war? This is peace? You're the peacemaker? You hear those sounds where Troy used to be? Those are Trojan slaves dismantling the walls of Troy, keeping pace with the whips lashing their backs. The Greeks won't leave one stone on top of another. There will be no ruins. They will obliterate all signs that Troy was ever here. And then they'll murder — sacrifice, they'll call it — all those workers. Only women will leave here alive, to bear their children or serve as drudges. Barbarians! Where are the gods? Where is their wrath?

"And here you are whole, unharmed, even happy, it would seem. The proud peacemaker. So why didn't they give you one of the Trojan women along with wealth and privilege, perhaps a small kingdom somewhere?"

"They offered me a pick of the spoils," he admits. "A high pick."

"And who did you take? Who did you choose to rape at your leisure? Anyone I know? A cousin perhaps? Or one of the palace handmaids?"

"I declined."

"How noble of you. Or did none of us suit your tastes? Did you pick a boy instead? A pretty lad, no doubt."

"There was one woman I wanted badly. But she was taken. And there was no one else I wanted, no one else I ever loved or could love."

"How sad for you to have caught that disease called *love*. It can get in the way of men abusing random women for their amusement. What's her name? And who owns her now?"

"Andromache. And Pyrrhus owns her."

"You joke. But you do so poorly. You're in love with me?" she laughs.

"You heard Cassandra's prophecy."

"That we would be together after Troy fell and would rule over some distant land? That was a joke, not a vision. Here I am bound like a goat ready for slaughter. And I'd be gagged and blindfolded as well but for your tender mercy, affording me the pleasure of cursing you out loud to your face and praying the gods to curse you — if only there were gods and justice."

"Calm. Please. You gain nothing by struggling against the ropes that bind you. I understand your grief. It will wane over time. And your anger will as well."

"Calm, you say? Calm? Here I am, the sex slave of a teenage madman who bashed the head of my infant son on the ramparts of Troy. Then he slit the throat of your sister Polyxena on the grave of his father, the one who killed Hector, my Hector, the only man I ever loved, or could ever love. And you ask me to be calm?"

Helenus leans close, to kiss her gently on the brow. She spits in his face — a large gob she must have been saving for such a moment. It hits him in the eye and drips down to his mouth.

"I'm sorry," he says.

"Really? Then all is forgiven."

"I'll be here with you."

"Here? Where is *here*? At anchor near the beach where once was Troy?

"With you. On the voyage to Greece, and even after that."

"What do you mean?"

"When I gave up my choice of spoils, I asked that Pyrrhus take me with you, not as his slave, but as his friend and companion."

"And Pyrrhus agreed to that? How gullible can you be?"

"Agamemnon agreed to those terms. I helped him when he needed help. He had Pyrrhus swear an oath on the grave of his father to treat me well and grant me this request. Admittedly, Pyrrhus is mad, but it's a superstitious madness. He thinks the shade of his father speaks to him. And he won't break an oath to his father."

"Well, you struck a bad bargain. He won't live long or I won't or both of us will die when I finally get my hands on him."

"No. You'll live. So Cassandra said. And I'll make sure that prophecy comes to pass. I'll protect you."

"Cassandra? You believe Cassandra? She doesn't believe herself anymore."

"You'll have a son."

"By Pyrrhus? You think I'd let that puny butcher put that thing of his in me? The first chance I get, I'll tear off whatever manhood he has stuff them down his throat. That's no figure of speech. That hope of sweet revenge is all that keeps me alive."

"He'll think the child is his. But I'll be the father."

"You're as mad as Pyrrhus."

"It's fated. Patience. I beg of you. The day will come when the two of us together will kill Pyrrhus. But no one will know that we did it, and we'll be free to marry, and we'll rule together in a distant land. And our son, Molossus ...

"Molossus?"

"Yes. Cassandra told me the name we should give him. And one day his descendant, our descendant, will conquer the world. And he'll dance naked on the grave of Achilles, dishonoring him for all time."

"You are as mad as your sister. But for that image, I could love you."

Chapter Six — Cassandra and Agamemnon

Signal fires alert Clytemnestra and Aegisthus a few hours after the Greeks win the war. But it's another year before Agamemnon arrives home.

By messenger, he explains again that he didn't sacrifice Iphie. That was never his intent. She slit her own throat. It was an accident. He should have gone home immediately to explain in person and to share his grief with her. He hadn't returned not just because of the wind, but also because he'd learned of her affair with Aegisthus. They'd been making a fool of him. None of his children were really his. At the time, he couldn't have controlled his temper. So he'd postponed the reckoning for after the war, never imagining it would last ten years.

Now he's a different man, from the experience of war, the passage of time, and the influence of another woman, Cassandra, daughter of King Priam of Troy. She has led him to realize he can and should forgive his wife and move on. Cassandra is a seer and knows their destiny.

He has his messenger say, "I've had enough of war. Now I want peace at any cost. I delayed my return because Cassandra was with child. Yesterday, she gave birth to twin boys, Teledamus and Pelops.

"I can now accept without bitterness that Orestes and Electra were fathered by Aegisthus, as was Iphigenia. You're free to marry Aegisthus. Let's end the blood feud. You and he can have Argos to rule. Take the children with you. On my return, in my new life as a new man, Cassandra will be my wife and the twins will be my heirs."

The voyage to Mycenae is like a marriage trip for Agamemnon and Cassandra.

To welcome them, Clytemnestra has the ground from the harbor to the palace covered with purple robes. As the returning king and his new wife follow that path, Cassandra carrying their sons, hundreds of children shower them with rose petals.

This is the beginning of a new life, a happy future.

Even before they've had a chance to discuss the details of what is to come — their sharing power, their future friendship — Clytemnestra acts kind and loving, not at all as Cassandra and Agamemnon expected.

"Here, let me take the babies," says Clytemnestra. "You must be tired, and they're so sweet."

"No need."

"But I insist." She takes them both and cradles them in her arms, bending and unbending her knees rhythmically, making faces at them, smiling at them, catching and holding their attention.

"They remind me of my own. At that age, they all look so much the same — boy, girl, prince, pauper. They remind me of my first, of Iphie. It's been so long. It's easy to forget. And I swore I'd never forget."

Cassandra hastens to say, "It didn't happen the way you think. He didn't do that. He couldn't."

"And you were there to see?"

"No. Of course not."

"And you didn't see that scene with your power of vision? You can't look into the past, only the future?"

"I can't see the future now. That plagued me for years, but it's over now."

"I don't need to be a prophet to know what happened. I have spies, many spies. And I know very well that Agamemnon slit my daughter's throat."

Cassandra objects, "But he didn't. I'm sure he didn't."

"And when you could see the future, did you see your own death?"

"No. I never did."

"A blind spot? What a shame. And here your twins are so lovely. And they look at each other as much as they look at me. Do you think they'll have a special bond with one another like you and your twin? Helen and I were never that close."

"Why did you speak of my death?"

"From the look in your eyes, you know what I mean. That was part of your vision, wasn't it?"

"That prophecy wasn't true," she insists.

"You didn't see it?"

"I did see it. But it didn't happen. Not everything in my vision happened."

"But it will, my dear. It will. We all die."

"But not that way."

"So you admit you did see it. You do know. You won't be surprised. You'd be surprised if it didn't happen."

"Why are you threatening me? Why be so cruel. I've never harmed you."

"I would never lift a hand against you. And I hold no ill will against you. You're not responsible for the deeds of your lover, nor am I for the deeds of mine. Aegisthus," she calls. "Come meet Cassandra. You'll like her. I'm sure we'll be great friends."

Cassandra turns to look. He's right behind her.

His knife is made of iron and has been sharpened so thin that she doesn't feel it as it slits her throat.

Chapter Seven — Helen in Arcadia

When Menelaus dies, Helen retires to Arcadia. There she composes a lengthy poem about her life and the war it caused. She writes it down, using Phoenician characters to represent Greek sounds. Only she knows how to read it.

Traveling bards visit her in Arcadia, learn the story by heart, and repeat it often, all over Greece. They add battle scenes and bloodshed — always crowd pleasers.

She remembers fondly the visit of Telemachus in search of his father and the look on Menelaus' face when she recounted that she walked three times around the hollow horse and knocked on its flanks and called out the names of the soldiers inside, mimicking the voices of their wives. That was the first time she added that detail.

Menelaus neither confirmed nor denied what she said, but she was sure he wanted to believe it. Her eyes flirted with his, inviting belief, but at the same time laughing at his gullibility.

In her written version, Menelaus tells that anecdote, implying that he's retelling what she told him, challenging the credulity of their guests.

She loves layering her narrative — one perspective on top of another, and none of them privileged and special, all possible at once.

She misses Menelaus. She misses Paris too, but she misses Menelaus more because he was the perfect audience, and a singer of tales needs an audience.

Remembering that scene with Telemachus reminds her of when Paris was his age. Back then, she didn't really know Menelaus and didn't know herself. If what happened after that hadn't happened, they would never have bonded as they finally did, and her life would have been much poorer.

Truth is dull and flat, she thinks, but story is alive, ever growing, ever changing, becoming ever more memorable. Anomalies and inconsistencies throw history into doubt, but they make story all the stronger. We want to believe all the more when we know that we can never be certain. Our confidence is an act of faith, an act of love.

Menelaus liked it when I told stories that couldn't be corroborated, when I told the same stories with variants, and no one knew which was *true* if any were.

He loved the way I could flirt with truth and flirt with him in doing so. In particular, he liked my telling of the story of the hollow horse. He believed he remembered the rhythmic knocking. It had to have been deliberate. Someone knew but didn't reveal that the horse was hollow, that there were warriors inside. Revelation could have led to the death of everyone in the horse and the Trojans might have saved their city.

Was that me knocking? He could never know that as a fact, but he believed it, even though he remembered not the sound of the knocking, but my telling of the tale.

His lingering doubt made his belief all the stronger, like belief in a god, like belief in all gods, like belief that life has meaning and that there is love and that my love for him was as strong as his for me.

*****

When bards visit and ask Helen to tell them her tale, she never shows them her written version. She doesn't try to teach any of them how to read it. Rather she forces them to rely on their memories, knowing that variations due to lapses of memory and creative twists added by retellers will make the story all the more memorable, through the narrative power of doubt.

Once a year, Helen visits Andromache and Helenus in Epirus. By chance, Cassandra's prophecy for them has turned out to be true. And perhaps many years hence there will be a namesake of Paris, a great Alexander who will conquer the world. So much that is impossible has happened already, why not that as well?

But she doesn't envy them their role in history. She will live in story, which lasts much longer than history and is far more fun to tell.

Printed in the USA
CPSIA information can be obtained
at www.ICGtesting.com
CBHW070827110524
8416CB00009B/455